A LOVELY TOUCH

Suncoast Society

Tymber Dalton

SIREN SENSATIONS

Siren Publishing, Inc.
www.SirenPublishing.com

A SIREN PUBLISHING BOOK
IMPRINT: Siren Sensations

A LOVELY SHADE OF OUCH
Copyright © 2015 by Tymber Dalton

ISBN: 978-1-63259-080-0

First Printing: March 2015

Cover design by Harris Channing
All art and logo copyright © 2015 by Siren Publishing, Inc.

ALL RIGHTS RESERVED: This literary work may not be reproduced or transmitted in any form or by any means, including electronic or photographic reproduction, in whole or in part, without express written permission.

All characters and events in this book are fictitious. Any resemblance to actual persons living or dead is strictly coincidental.

Printed in the U.S.A.

PUBLISHER
Siren Publishing, Inc.
www.SirenPublishing.com

AUTHOR'S NOTE

This book features Gilo and Abbey, and events toward the beginning of this book overlap slightly with events at the end of *His Canvas* (Suncoast Society 10). While the books in the Suncoast Society series are standalone works which may be read independently of each other, the recommended reading order to avoid spoilers is as follows:

1. *Safe Harbor*
2. *Cardinal's Rule*
3. *Domme by Default*
4. *The Reluctant Dom*
5. *The Denim Dom*
6. *Pinch Me*
7. *Broken Toy*
8. *A Clean Sweep*
9. *A Roll of the Dice*
10. *His Canvas*
11. *A Lovely Shade of Ouch*

Some of the minor characters who appear in this book also appear in other books in the Suncoast Society series. All titles are available from Siren-BookStrand

A LOVELY SHADE OF OUCH

Suncoast Society

TYMBER DALTON
Copyright © 2015

Chapter One

John Gilomen sat and stared at his computer screen, trying to make sense of his office e-mail.

Wasn't working.

Nothing seemed to want to work in his brain at that exact moment. Not when he'd just been hammered by the news that a dear friend of his since high school had died.

He took off his glasses and set them on his desk. Leaning back in his chair, he rubbed at his eyes. No, he wasn't going to sit there and bawl like a baby. Not at work.

Worst. Thursday. Ever.

He hadn't even known Mick was having a problem, but it had happened suddenly. Went in for a routine colonoscopy yesterday morning, and earlier this morning, he'd died from peritonitis.

Shit.

John had just eaten dinner with Mick and Mick's wife, Nancy, a couple of weeks earlier. Mick had been one of the few people from high school he'd kept in touch with, over twenty-five years since their graduation. And even rarer in numbers from that small pool, they'd both settled in the Sarasota area, not far from where they'd grown up.

Mick had gone to college at UF in Gainesville and become an

ophthalmologist. John had majored in engineering at USF in Tampa and now worked for Manasota Electric Co-op as their head safety engineer.

Breathe through it.

While that worked perfectly for dealing with physical pain, handling emotional pain was a totally different beast.

Which was why he usually preferred to deal with physical pain. It faded fairly quickly.

His cell phone still lay on his desk. Nancy had called him in tears a few minutes earlier. Nancy and her kids had plenty of family surrounding them right at that moment. He didn't want to race over and intrude.

Then there was the fact that he honestly didn't know how to deal with his own emotions. The last thing Nancy would need was for him to burst into tears in front of her. She needed people around her she was closer to, who could be strong for her. He knew and liked Nancy, but he was friends with Mick.

Had been.

Shit.

The knock on his open office door startled him, nearly sending him off-balance in the chair when he turned around.

Dell Clayburne from Communications stood there as John worked to get himself situated.

"You all right?" Dell looked amused.

Why deny it? "No, I'm not."

Dell's face fell as John explained. "Oh, man. I'm so sorry. I didn't mean to sound like a dick."

"It's okay. You didn't know."

"You going to take off?"

"There's nothing I can do for his wif—widow right now. They've got grown kids, family, other friends. I'd just be in the way." He settled his glasses back on his face. He only needed them for computer work, so far. "What'd you need?"

Dell held a sheaf of papers in his hands. "No, this can wait. I just wanted to go through some stuff with you before I get interviewed by Bay News 9 late tomorrow morning about that incident on Tuesday."

The "incident" being a contractor doing work on their Bradenton power plant had accidentally hung himself while performing work on one of the large stacks.

John arched an eyebrow at him. "Then I don't think it can wait, can it?"

"I mean…" Dell rubbed at his face. "I'm sorry. You really should go take care of your personal stuff."

John held out a hand for the papers. "Let's do it now. If Nancy does need me, I probably won't have another chance later. And I don't know if I'll even be in tomorrow. I'd rather go through it with you while I can and not have anyone from legal crawling up my rear end for not doing it."

"You sure?"

"I'm sure. Grab a chair and let's see what you've got."

* * * *

John ended up leaving work at lunchtime. He needed time to get his head together, to think, to process. He couldn't begin to contemplate facing Nancy and her kids until he'd done that much.

He grabbed a sandwich and a drink from Subway and headed over to the De Soto National Memorial park, which was only twenty minutes from his office. On a weekday this time of year, they wouldn't be very busy.

Fortunately, they weren't. He parked in the shade before walking out to a bench that overlooked the mouth of the Manatee River where it dumped into the southern end of Tampa Bay. There, he tried to quiet his mind, tried not to overthink things as he forced himself to eat.

It'd be too easy to settle into a dark place emotionally. Better to lock things away.

Although, without the stark grief of Mick's wife and other family right in front of him, it was still too easy to stay detached from it. From his own emotional pain.

While he was good at many things, dealing with emotional pain wasn't one of them.

Physical pain, on the other hand, he was a master of that. Enjoyed owning and controlling the way he dealt with it. Enjoyed how it could temporarily transport his mind to a blissful place where he was able to shove everything else aside except the pain. Loved working with the pain from the inside out, like a potter with clay, molding it, forming it, transforming it into something useful until he came out on the other side of it.

He knew what he had to do that afternoon, he just didn't *want* to do it.

Not entirely accurate. He wanted to go be a support for Nancy and the kids, but wasn't sure he could be one. And he didn't want to add to her misery when the expectation of his presence would likely be to comfort her, her two sons, and her daughter.

One part of himself he didn't like, but at least he owned it. Understood his limitations.

Why is this kind of shit so easy for other people?

Finding a therapist to talk to wouldn't help. He'd tried that before. Trying to explain to a shrink that he'd rather get his balls kicked than face a personal, emotional loss usually earned him strange looks and the therapist's desire to find the root cause buried in the trauma that had caused the disconnect.

Fuck that noise.

He *knew* the cause.

What he wanted to know was the cure. Thus far, no one had offered one to him that didn't involve suggestions of medication and talk therapy that was utter bullshit. Mental masturbation of the not-fun kind.

Not when he could go to the club and get his ass caned and find a little bit of respite there, even if it didn't provide a resolution.

He wanted to know the way others dealt with shit. But to hear a counselor say "they just deal with it in their own way" was neither helpful nor productive. And tossing suggestions for "normal" stuff at him that he'd already tried—and failed at—wasn't helpful or productive, either.

He already had a way he dealt with it.

He wanted a *better* way to deal with it.

At forty-five, he suspected he wasn't going to find a better way to deal with it if he hadn't already.

Maybe I'm overthinking it.

Okay, no maybes about it, he was definitely overthinking it. He overthought a lot of things.

Most things.

Hence why getting the crap beaten out of him from time to time allowed him to shut down the thinking processes for a little while.

And here I am avoiding the issue by sitting here and staring at my navel and whining in my head about how I can't deal with shit.

Like the fact that my best friend is dead.

He thought about calling Seth, but he didn't know if the good-natured man would appreciate being asked something like that.

Hey, how'd you deal with Kaden dying?

Even though it had been a few years since Kaden's death, Seth probably wouldn't appreciate an out-of-the-blue question like that.

Not to mention it was a totally different situation there. Seth and Leah had time to prepare themselves. Kaden himself had made extensive preparations for his wife and best friend before he died, to ease them through the process. Vanilla and kinky preparations.

Hell, Mick was his best friend, but even he hadn't even known about the kinky parts of John's life. John never mixed the vanilla and the kink. There was too much personally at stake for him to do that. He didn't think he could lose his job over it but it might make things extremely uncomfortable for him at work if this aspect of his life ever became common knowledge.

Maybe Tony could offer me some advice.

Then again, Tony was a full-on Dom. That might not be any help at all, even though he was friends with the man.

Maybe Essie can offer me advice.

She'd been estranged from her parents when her father died.

Then again, he didn't know her a fraction as well as he knew Tony or Seth.

This is what I get for being a loner. Maybe I deserve this. Maybe this is some sort of karmic retribution I don't even know about.

That would be easier to believe if he had a belief system to start with.

He'd learned at an early age that, sometimes, bad things happen to good people. That shit happens.

It. Just. Happens.

The way it had happened to Mick, someone who'd lived a good life, had a great wife and family, someone who'd been active in community and charity organizations like the Lions and Rotary.

Someone who didn't deserve to die over something as stupid as a routine health procedure designed to catch and prevent future health issues.

Horrific irony.

If something like that happened to John, he really didn't have any next of kin to notify. No girlfriend, no close relatives, no siblings.

Not even a dog or cat to worry about or miss him if he didn't come home.

He imagined someone at work would begin to wonder where he was if he didn't show up and call in, but other than that...

Jesus, I'm pitiful.

After a few more minutes, he gathered his trash, tossed it in a garbage can on his way to the car, and headed home to change clothes and decide how to handle the next, excruciating part of his day.

Chapter Two

Late Thursday morning, Abbey Rockland sat in her car outside the orthopedic surgeon's office and cried following her appointment. Not just from the pain in her back, which was excruciating, but also from frustration.

Surgery was inevitable if she wanted her life back. The freak fall she'd taken at work eight weeks earlier, when she and several coworkers had decided to take the stairs two flights down to go to a meeting in a conference room on a different floor instead of waiting for an elevator, had resulted in two blown disks in her lower back.

There weren't any other options. Physical therapy would only delay the inevitable without providing her any results or relief.

That the doctor recommended she get a cane and use it to help her get around until after the surgery had been yet another blow to her psyche.

She'd been working limited hours ever since the accident, which had hit her wallet far harder than she'd expected. Workmen's comp didn't cover the full amount of pay she lost, either.

Another shocker.

The only good thing so far was that WC was paying for all her medical expenses. Their company's health care plan was okay, but had this happened to her outside of work, she would have been screwed because of co-pays.

After the surgery, the doctor told her to expect to be out of work a minimum of four weeks, more likely six to eight weeks. Even then, when she returned to work, she'd be on restricted hours again for several more weeks.

Meaning even more of a hit to her wallet. Hits she couldn't afford right now. Not with her boyfriend, Tom, unable to find another decent job in the area after the local hardware store chain he'd worked for had sold out to a national chain. He'd been half of their in-house IT department, which was phased out and taken over by the new, larger corporate owner.

Laid off, no one in the area wanted to touch the previous salary he'd made, and his unemployment was close to running out. At least her job as a senior operations research analyst was secure. The firm she worked for had steadily grown over the eleven years she'd been there, with a bright future on the horizon. She managed ten people on two different teams. That was in addition to handling a couple of accounts personally, clients who'd started with her and had requested she remain in charge of their ongoing projects following her promotions.

Deep breaths, Abbey. Deep breaths.

They were renting the house they lived in. Technically, it was Tom's house, because she'd moved in with him four years earlier and had given up her apartment. Her car was paid for. She had practically no credit card debt.

Yet.

She pulled herself together and winced as she moved her seat forward a little to make it easier to drive. She could have asked Tom to bring her, but he'd been going out on another round of interviews today and she didn't want to do anything to ruin that for him.

Maybe I should have gotten the script for painkillers filled.

She'd been getting by on over-the-counter painkillers, a heating pad, homeopathic salves, and her TENS unit. The TENS unit had never been used for nonkinky play before her back injury.

Now, it proved a godsend. The pain relief it gave her, while temporary, was better than anything else.

She'd had a bad reaction to painkillers in college, when she'd needed a root canal after a tooth abscessed. Since then, she'd sworn never to take them again.

The pain she'd experienced since her fall had nearly been enough to make her rethink her pledge about painkillers, but not quite. Even though she was used to doling out pain, not experiencing it, she was tough. She'd had her fair share of canings and paddlings over the years until she realized she was a Dominant, not a bottom.

Tom had been sympathetic and doing his best to take up the slack around the house, but she felt badly that she hadn't had the energy or the desire to play with him at all since her fall. The last thing she'd felt was sexy or dominant.

There were times it'd been all she could do to not burst into tears in front of him.

Carefully, she made her way home, taking a moment in the driveway before pulling herself out of the car.

I'm forty-one and I feel like I'm eighty-one.

Life wasn't supposed to be like this. Yes, Tom's unexpected career derailment had proven to be a bump in the road, but shit happened. She still had her job, a good job, and she had faith he'd find something else. Things had been going fairly well between them even though their sex life had dwindled. She attributed it to the stress he felt over his job loss. Understandable.

And then her stupid accident.

They'd never talked marriage. When they first got together, Tom was recovering from a wicked divorce from a woman who'd cheated on him and driven him into credit card debt behind his back.

Abbey had decided long ago she wasn't exactly the marrying kind. Not that she had anything against it in theory, but between her parents' nasty divorce, and her brother and sister both going through nasty divorces, she decided it was easier not to have that entanglement.

In the almost five years she'd been with Tom, counting the time before they moved in together, the topic of marriage had never come up beyond her telling him she didn't want that, and him agreeing.

They didn't even have a joint bank account.

She slowly walked into the house, setting her purse on the table in the front hall, and then made her way out onto the lanai.

"Hey, George." Carefully lowering herself into a chair on the screened-in lanai, she stared at the large enclosure for her Russian tortoise. "How was your day, buddy?"

He'd completely muddied his water dish, but she wasn't sure if she could bend down to pick it up right then. Sometimes she could, and sometimes she had to have Tom do it. Since this was Sarasota, George could live in his lanai enclosure most of the year. Four feet wide and eight feet long, it was made from two-by-eight planks, two planks high, with mesh weed-barrier fabric stapled to the bottom of it so the dirt—and George—couldn't get out. Also, rainwater could drain out. It was positioned half under the roof's overhang so there was shelter and shade from the sun, in addition to his cozy tortoise house. She'd planted sod, as well as tortoise-safe plants, inside the enclosure for him to graze on.

She also had a small plastic kiddie pool she used for him as an inside enclosure when it was too chilly or otherwise inclement for him to be outside.

George—named for her crush on George Clooney when she was in college—was twenty-one years old, and probably the closest thing she'd ever have to a baby.

Well, scratch that, George *was* her baby. Her college roommate had been allergic to dogs and cats, and Abbey had wanted a pet. A friend told her about another friend, whose parents raised tortoises and turtles…

And she'd fallen in love with the little hatchling.

Now he was about ten inches long, as large as he'd ever get.

Tom hadn't been too thrilled with George, but had agreed with little complaint. He'd even helped her put together the enclosure, something she'd not been able to do for George before with apartment living. He'd spent his days in his kiddie pool on her screened balcony while she was at work, and she let him roam the apartment in the evening when she returned home.

George had lifted his head when he heard her speak to him and was now slowly shambling toward where she sat at the shaded end of the enclosure.

"You're kind of walking the way I'm feeling," she joked. "Just shuffling along, sort of slow."

The tortoise made his way to the corner closest to her, craning his neck as he looked up expectantly.

"Oh, dang it. Sorry, buddy. Hold on." Wincing, she pushed up and out of the chair and went inside to the fridge, pulling out a few pieces of baby romaine lettuce. His enclosure had enough established plants in it that she didn't have to supplement his food during the summer months.

But every tortoise loves their treats, and in her pain, and her self-pity over finding out about needing surgery, she'd forgotten their daily ritual.

She returned to the lanai, pulled the chair over to the side of the enclosure, and heavily sat again. "Okay, buddy. Here you go." She ripped off small pieces of romaine and held them out for George to nibble on.

George was always a calming influence on her, very Zen. Whenever she felt stressed, or overwhelmed, or frantic, all she had to do was spend some time contemplating the little guy's peaceful existence.

Which was something few people knew about her.

I'm the Tortoise Talker.

She chuckled a little at that thought. "I guess you and I will be spending some quality time together after my surgery."

Inside the house, she heard the front door open and close. She hadn't been paying attention, had missed the sound of Tom's car pulling into the driveway out front. When she saw him round the corner, she waved to him through the sliders.

He stepped outside to join her.

From the look on his face, she could tell things hadn't gone well. "Are you all right?" she asked.

He didn't answer at first. Instead, he pulled another chair over to where she sat feeding George. "His water's muddy."

"I know. I'm sorry, but can you please—"

"Yeah." He stood, reached into the enclosure, grabbed the large terra cotta plant dish, and carried it outside to the spigot. There he rinsed it out, refilled it, and brought it back, replacing it in the enclosure.

"Thank you," she quietly said.

"Yeah. No problem." He wouldn't make eye contact with her as he returned to the other chair.

Something deep inside her twisted in a bad way.

Worse, she didn't know what to say to break the tension.

She handed George another piece of romaine.

Tom finally took a deep breath. "What'd the doctor say?"

She felt bad about saddling Tom with this, too. "Surgery. The MRIs were pretty conclusive."

"But workman's comp pays all that, right?"

"Yeah."

He slowly nodded. "Okay. That's good."

"Yeah."

"How long will you be laid up after?"

"Depends on how I heal. Anywhere from four to eight weeks."

"Is it scheduled yet?"

She handed George another piece of lettuce. That twisting sensation deep inside her was about to snap her nerves clean off. Tom seemed to be building up to something but she wasn't sure what.

"They're going to call me. The woman who sets up his surgical schedule was out today. Probably at least three weeks or so before they do it. He wasn't sure."

Tom still wouldn't meet her gaze. "Yeah."

After a couple of minutes, just when she thought she'd have to outright ask him what was going on, he spoke again. "Do you want the good news, or the bad news?"

Despite the heat of the day, a chill settled inside her. "You pick." She kept her focus on George, unable to look at Tom.

"Ab, there's no way to say this other than to say it. This isn't working out for me. I was hoping to stick around until after you were back on your feet, but I got a job offer today. It's out in Dallas."

The chill turned into a full-blown blizzard as she sensed her emotions getting just as lost in the white-out. "Okay?"

"I already called the landlord, told him what's up. He said he'd let me out of the lease early."

She didn't answer. She wanted him to get all the way through it. She'd hoped this wasn't as bad as she thought it would be, but her common sense told her otherwise.

Ever since her accident, she'd felt Tom pulling away from her. Maybe even before that, but especially since. She'd offered to help him get off in bed despite her own lack of desire due to her pain. He'd rebuffed her efforts, their intimacy dropping to nil as he rolled over with his back to her every night after coming to bed late.

She hadn't snooped, thought it beneath her.

Still, inside, she'd suspected.

Things had changed ever since her accident, and it wasn't just because she could barely function through her vanilla life. Their kinky life was totally nonexistent at this point even though he had hinted at playing a couple of times despite refusing sex.

"I'm going to fly out on Monday to go through training and stuff and find a place to live. I'll be back next Friday night."

George was being a little piggy with his lettuce today. She ripped off another small piece and handed it to him.

"I'm going to need you to move out, Abbey. I know you can't afford to live here by yourself. Unless you get a roommate or something, and if you want to do that, then let me know and we'll go transfer the lease into your name with the landlord and handle the utilities and stuff."

"Who is she?" Abbey didn't realize she'd actually whispered the words out loud until she finally looked at Tom again and saw his shock. Like she'd slapped him.

That he didn't immediately deny it told her all she needed to know. She wasn't going to interrogate him if he wouldn't answer, but he surprised her again and volunteered the details.

"You don't know her. I met her on FetLife. She lives out there. I haven't met her in real life yet, don't even know if there will be anything between us. But I was looking through job listings and stuff out there while she and I were messaging back and forth. I applied to a couple of places and a recruiter called me. I did a Skype interview with their HR department the other day and they made me an offer today. The starting salary is only five thousand less than what I was making, full benefits, retirement plan, every—"

"How long until I have to be out?" she quietly asked, hating that this had been going on for a while and she'd been so out of it she hadn't even been able to pick up on it.

"Look, yes, I love you, and I'm sorry as hell to have to do this to you, but I can't handle this. I thought I could, and maybe it makes me a shit to bail, but I need to do what's best for me. It doesn't mean I don't care about you. I'll always love and care about you, but it's time for me to move on."

"You're right." She returned her focus to George. It stung more that he said he loved her. She would have preferred it if he'd told her he'd fallen out of love with her. Would have made the news easier to take.

"As soon as you find a place, I'll help you move," he quickly continued. "I'll do all the packing for you. I'll pay for a truck, everything. I know I owe you that much. It's just that between the job situation, and now your health, you know as well as I do that part of your life is over. I need a strong Dominant. It's not your fault and I'm not blaming you, but people change. You've changed, and you're not the person I need. I need to start over. If Dallas is where I need to do it, okay, then that's where I'll do it. Life is short. Damn short."

"Yeah."

Thank god I'm not married to him.

That irony slammed home hard, nearly starting her tears.

She dug the nails of her right hand into her palm, trying to shut off the waterworks. No way in hell would she do that, cry in front of him.

Nope.

No way she'd give him the satisfaction.

He'd never once mentioned job hunting outside of Florida. Sure, they'd discussed what might have to happen if he found a good-paying job, say over on the east coast, or south in Naples or something.

But not out of state.

She couldn't, wouldn't uproot herself. She had too many years invested in her job, had too many friends here. Even her family, as whacked-out and dysfunctional as they were, had remained tethered to the Sarasota area.

"Do I need to get tested?" she asked.

"No, I swear, I haven't slept with anyone but you since we've been together. And I don't know if it'll work out with her, anyway. We haven't even met yet. I never cheated on you."

It took every last ounce of willpower for her not to laugh in his face. He hadn't cheated on her?

Suuure.

Cheating took many forms, not just physical.

That he didn't understand that basic principle drove home how incompatible they were.

Maybe this is for the best, before I wasted more time with him.

"Okay," she quietly said.

He finally went inside. After she finished feeding George his treat, she regretted she couldn't get down on her hands and knees to play with him, to tidy up his enclosure, to lay eye-to-eye with him on the ground while she stroked his head with her finger, something he loved when she did it.

It took her a good twenty minutes or so to finally be sure she wouldn't break down into tears. Then she slowly stood and went into the kitchen to wash her hands. Without knowing exactly where she was going to go, she made her way to the foyer, grabbed her purse and her keys, and left the house.

Chapter Three

John unlocked his front door, switched off the alarm, and went inside. Locking the door behind him, he resisted the urge to go straight to the fridge and pull out a bottle of beer.

He hadn't yet decided how to handle Nancy. He'd called her again before leaving work early. Her eldest son, Paul, had answered the phone and assured John he was welcome to come over if he wanted to. But upon pressing a little further, John also found out she had a house full of people at that time.

Personally, he didn't want to intrude.

And he wasn't sure how to handle his grief around a bunch of people he didn't know.

Isn't that why I became a freak to begin with?

Okay, no, not a freak. But it didn't take a psychiatrist to tell him that his masochism stemmed from his childhood trauma, of being unable to process and openly express emotions in a safe place at a time when he most needed to.

Yet if pressed, he also wouldn't call himself broken. People had dealt with worse than he had and come out even better than him. All things considered, he was a well-adjusted, successful, self-supporting, financially stable person.

That he liked to get the crap beaten out of him to help get rid of emotions he didn't want to deal with was a nontraditional coping mechanism, sure, but it worked even if he sometimes wished he didn't need it.

If it ain't broke, don't fix it, I guess.

If he didn't go visit her today, he'd likely feel guilty as hell over it. And if she did want him there, he'd feel even guiltier about it in retrospect.

Guilt…or grief?

It was a tough call to make, but he finally settled on grief. He changed out of his work clothes into jeans and a button up shirt and headed out again.

On the way, he stopped at a Publix to pick up a condolence card and a sandwich platter. He didn't know if they'd need the food or not, but at least it was something.

As he passed one aisle, he stopped. Turning, he went down it and scooped six boxes of tissues into his cart.

They would definitely need those. After a little more thought, he picked up plastic cups, paper plates, and paper towels. And a package of garbage bags. With the inundation of visitors, it'd be easier on them to not have to wash dishes every time they turned around. Large numbers of people always meant large numbers of trash.

He returned to the deli and grabbed another sandwich platter, just in case.

By the time he reached the register, he'd also added a couple of cases of soda, a bag of ice, and a case of bottled water.

It wasn't comfort, but maybe it would help in some small way.

When John arrived at their house just north of Osprey, in a rural neighborhood, the driveway and yard were full of cars and several more had been parked along the street. He grabbed the card and the two sandwich platters and walked up to the front door. He didn't even have to knock, because Paul had already opened the door for him as he walked up.

He clumsily hugged John. "Thank you for coming."

"I'm really sorry."

"Thanks." He took the sandwich platters from him. "Come on in. Mom will be happy to see you."

"I need to get some other groceries out of my car first. I brought drinks and stuff."

"Oh, hey, thank you. We were going to send someone out. I'll come help you." He foisted the sandwich platters off on a woman John didn't know and followed him outside.

"How's your mom holding up?" It felt like a dumb question, but one he was supposed to ask.

"Not good. I don't think any of us are. It was a shock."

John unlocked his car and, without rumpling the card, managed to help Paul get the rest of the stuff out and into the house in one trip.

Matt, their youngest at seventeen, was in the kitchen and helped them put things away.

"Mom's out on the lanai," Paul said. "Come on out." He started leading him that way.

John knew the way, had been here countless times in the past. Nancy looked horrible, as expected. Heartbroken, grief-stricken, her eyes red, nose swollen from crying, her hair a mess.

She stood when she spotted him, practically falling into his arms. "What am I going to do, John?" she softly keened. "What am I going to do without him?"

He held her as she sobbed against his chest, Paul taking the card from him and carrying it inside.

John knew the right words to say, the motions to make, the expressions to hold on his face.

Inside, he felt the walls descending, stony, hard, cold. The emotional watertight compartments slamming shut and separating that part of him from the rest of his world.

He also knew, sooner rather than later, he'd need a good beating to short-circuit that and deal with it. If not, it would seep into other areas of his life, until he wouldn't be able to sleep, concentrate, focus.

Function.

Not until he dealt with it.

"I'm so sorry," he whispered as he hugged her. "I don't know what to say."

That much was true. He was still trying to deal with the reality that his friend wasn't just upstairs and missing out on the gathering below.

He didn't know what to say to her, because he wasn't even sure what *he* would do yet with Mick gone from his life.

After a few minutes, she peeled herself off him and someone John thought he recognized from previous gatherings as a friend of Nancy's pressed tissues into her hand.

"We're going to have a memorial on Saturday morning at ten," Nancy said. "At Moalen Brothers in downtown Sarasota. He wanted to be cremated."

"Okay. Is there anything I can do to help? Is there anything you need?"

She looked around, bereft, lost. She shrugged, then nodded, then shook her head and burst into tears again. It was open his arms to her or have her fall against him.

Finally, about fifteen minutes later, more of her family arrived including her brother, allowing John to tactfully untangle himself from her and escape to the backyard.

This had been Mick's pride and joy, besides his family. He loved gardening and landscaping.

Taking a deep breath, John felt a wave of nausea sweep through him. He bent over and put his hands on his knees, knowing it would pass soon enough.

This doesn't feel real.

He wished it was a nightmare he could awaken from, but the worst things in life usually weren't. He'd rather choose a truckload of monsters from the darkest recesses of his subconscious chasing him through sleep every night over having to deal with this.

Once he knew his stomach had steadied, he returned to the house, glad that, for now, Nancy seemed to be engulfed by other friends and family. Matt stood in the kitchen, intently staring at one of the sandwich platters as if trying to make an earth-shattering decision about it.

"Hey." John wasn't sure what else to say. His own situation had been so different than this, from start to bloody, tragic end. "I'm sorry. I don't know what to say."

Matt nodded. His eyes were also red, but he looked like maybe he'd gone from crying to numb, while his mom was still trying to process what had happened.

John offered him a hand, to shake with him. But the boy didn't let go, and then dipped his head, his shoulders silently shaking.

Okay, so maybe not numb.

John hugged him, the boy crying as silently as his mother was now loudly sobbing again somewhere in the vicinity of the living room. He knew the boy should be out there, with his mom and older brother and sister, and other family, but didn't have the heart to make him move yet.

And John knew the things he *couldn't* say to him, things on the tip of his tongue that would sound so wrong if said aloud, but would be meant well.

At least you still have your mom.

At least you have older siblings.

At least you're seventeen, and not twelve.

At least your dad didn't beat your mom to a pulp, and then she shot him after he got drunk, and then she shot herself.

At least you didn't walk in on it.

At least you didn't have to call the cops.

At least...

Perspective that would neither be appropriate nor warranted. This kid was the victim of a different kind of tragedy, whether malpractice or misfortune as yet to be seen, he supposed.

The irreversible result remained the same. Matt would start college next fall. This was his senior year of high school, supposed to be the best time of his life before the next stage started.

And now...

The boy sniffled a little and pulled away, quickly turning to rip a piece of paper towel off the roll next to the kitchen sink. After blowing his nose, he washed his face. Only then did he turn back to John.

"Thanks," he quietly said. Then he walked out of the kitchen.

John stared at the sandwich platters, wishing they held answers.

* * * *

More family, friends, and coworkers poured into the house, stuffing it nearly to bursting. John made sure to give all three kids a hug, and then Nancy, before excusing himself just before dark fell. Too much grief, too much visible suffering in the faces and voices, Nancy's renewed cries every time someone else arrived and she was forced to tell the story again.

Necessary for her process. Necessary for her grief to flow and not get bottled up to rot her from the inside out.

John's grief process had taken a different route long ago. His was like slow-flowing lava, cooling and leaving cold stone in its wake. All he could do was seal off the compartments until he could chip away at it later, once it was safe to handle.

Once it no longer possessed the ability to burn him from the inside out.

He stopped by a liquor store on the way home and picked up a bottle of rum and a two-liter bottle of Coke.

Mick's favorite drink.

John wasn't much of a drinker, not even in college. He'd had to work too hard and had too much to prove.

Now…

Now he was successful by all the usual benchmarks. Owned his house, owned his car, had a great job he could conceivably retire from eventually, as long as he didn't commit any massive fuckups in the next several years.

Mick had been the one person who'd known the full truth about his life. About that night. About what had happened.

Everyone else knew his parents had died when he was twelve, and he'd come to Sarasota to live with his father's parents.

No one else knew what had happened out in Los Angeles. That had been before the Internet really became a thing every kid his age had access to. Not like today. Now, someone could easily go onto Google and plug in his parents' names and come up with if not the newspaper articles, then at least a police report, or vital statistics documents stating their manner of death.

Homicide and suicide.

He'd told people they were from Atlanta, which wasn't a lie because they'd lived there until the disastrous year in California. His dad had moved them out there for a job, but his drinking got worse when he'd lost it. And his temper got worse.

Until that final night.

By the time John got home it was full dark. He made himself a tall glass with ice, added Coke to the halfway point, then finished it off with rum. Stripping, he walked out to the hot tub on his lanai and climbed in. The benefit of an eight-foot privacy fence around the backyard, he could skinny dip in his pool or hot tub whenever he wanted.

Without any lights on along the lanai, he could look up and see stars in the sky. As he lifted his glass, he contemplated what to say. He wasn't a religious person, and neither was Mick.

"I'm going to miss you, man," he finally said. "Going to miss the bullshit sessions that went on till midnight, going to miss the phone calls on my birthday. Going to miss you."

He downed half the glass, waiting a moment for the inevitable belch as the soda worked its way through his digestive tract.

"That was a good one, huh?"

An old joke between them.

With Mick in his life, even though they didn't talk every day, he hadn't felt quite so…alone. Yes, he had coworkers and distant relatives and acquaintances. Even a few people who knew about a small part of his life, again compartmentalized by necessity but for a different reason, that no one else knew about.

And he was still alone.

With Mick gone, he was a little more alone than before.

John sat back in the hot tub and downed the rest of his drink before setting the glass on the edge, leaning his head back, and staring up at the cold, distant, silent stars.

Chapter Four

Abbey wasn't sure where she was going at first, until she realized she was heading toward Tilly's house. She almost drove past Tilly's driveway and kept going, but knew her best friend would be upset if she didn't come to her now, of all times.

I've hit rock bottom.

That was exactly what it felt like when she parked behind Tilly's SUV and shut the car off.

Abbey sat there for a moment, working up the strength to endure the painful struggle to get out of the car when Tilly's front door opened. Cris appeared, with a curious look on his face, followed by a frown as he stepped outside, closed the door behind him, and walked down the driveway to her car.

She opened the door.

"Abbey? What's wrong?"

The tears started, sobs wracking her body. Then she heard Cris yelling for Tilly and Landry, and he was gently getting her out of the car after unfastening her seat belt for her. Abbey was still sobbing as Tilly and Landry joined them, the three of them helping her inside and to their sofa.

Tilly, a former nurse who'd been closely following her friend's health ordeal, gently held her, rocking her as Landry sat on Abbey's other side.

"Sweetie, what's wrong?" Tilly asked. "What happened?"

Cris disappeared for a moment and reappeared with a box of tissues, pressing a couple of them into Abbey's hand. It took her a few minutes, but Abbey finally got everything out. From her news about needing surgery to the bombshell Tom had just dropped on her.

"That son of a bitch," Tilly muttered. "I'll fucking castrate him my—"

"Love," Landry interrupted. "I don't think revenge fantasies are appropriate at this juncture."

Abbey managed a bitter, snot-filled laugh. "And if you castrate him, he won't be able to move my shit. Not that I have any idea where I'm going to move *to* yet."

"Don't worry, babe," Tilly said. "You're moving in here, with us."

"I appreciate that, but don't you think your guys should get a say in that?"

"We don't need a say," Cris said. "You're moving in here." He looked at Landry, who nodded.

"Agreed," Landry said.

Tears threatened to overwhelm her again. "Thank you, guys, really, but I can't impose on you like that."

"Where else are you going to go?" Tilly asked. "You'll probably be in the hospital at least two nights, maybe three. When you get home, you'll need help. What better place than here? We can store your furniture in the garage so you don't have to pay a storage fee. Then, once you're healed, we'll all help you move to wherever you're going."

"You guys have a life and jobs."

"Yeah, so?" Cris said. "Tilly's either home during the day, or doing volunteer stuff with Leah and Loren. And she's a nurse. It's perfect. She can drive you to your appointments and everything."

"What about George?"

Tilly frowned. "George?" Then realization set in. "Oh, your turtle. He can move in, too. No worries."

"Tortoise. I'll have to keep him in my room." They didn't have a screened lanai big enough for his enclosure, and she didn't want to keep him out in the open because of mosquitoes and other insects, or predators, like raccoons, dogs, or cats.

Landry took over. "George is welcomed in our home."

Abbey didn't have the energy to fight them. She knew her friends meant well, and she loved them for it. "Okay." Despite her best efforts, she started crying again. "Thank you."

"Do you want to stay here with us tonight?" Tilly asked. "I'll drive you back home and—"

"No," Cris and Landry vehemently said, actually bringing a small smile to Abbey's face.

"Not about the staying here part," Landry quickly amended. "But if anyone goes back with her, it'll be myself or Cris. *Not* you."

"Why not me?" Tilly indignantly asked.

"Because you'll end up needing to be bailed out of jail," Cris said. "You've got a temper, sweetheart. You can't deny that."

Yes, Tilly did have a temper. But as large as her temper was, her heart and her love for her friends were even bigger, by a thousand times.

Tilly wrinkled her nose at her men. "Okay, *fine*."

"Your choice," Landry told Abbey. "You are welcomed to stay starting tonight. I'll talk to the others and get a moving committee arranged for this weekend."

Abbey thought about how their friends had rallied around Mallory when she'd needed to move, literally an emergency, out of the house she'd shared with her uncle. He'd been threatening her, and Tilly had been the first to arrive on the scene to back the uncle down until everyone else could get there.

They'd moved her out in about an hour, although she'd just had a bedroom's worth of furniture, not half of a house. And they'd had at least eight people helping.

In fact, Mallory and Askel's collaring ceremony was that weekend.

Now, Abbey didn't know if she even had the heart to go.

"I have to work tomorrow," she said. "Maybe it's better if I just go home tonight and come back Saturday."

"Are you sure?" Tilly asked. "I mean it, it's okay."

"I know. And I appreciate it. But I need to pack. And get stuff ready for George. And..." She choked back another round of tears.

"Change of plans, then," Tilly said. "I'll stay at your house tomorrow night and help you with all of that—"

"Love," Landry interrupted. "You're forgetting your role on Saturday."

Tilly winced. "Shit. Okay, scratch that. *After* the collaring on Saturday, we'll coordinate the effort to get you moved and Sunday we'll actually move you. How's *that* sound?"

"I don't know if I can even go on Saturday. I've been spending weekends recovering from work. Driving hurts like hell."

"No, you *will* go. We'll come pick you up on our way there so you don't even have to drive." Tilly scowled. "Is Tom going?"

"I don't know. He didn't say he wasn't. He was invited. Maybe he won't go now. I don't know."

Cris laughed. "Well, when you tell him Tilly's picking you up Saturday, he might decide to uninvite himself."

"If he's smart," Landry added. "If he's brilliant, he'll make himself scarce all day Saturday and Sunday."

"No," Tilly darkly added, "he's a fucking moron. If he was smart, he wouldn't be acting like a such a goddamned dick."

* * * *

Tilly insisted Abbey was staying for dinner. And, Tilly added, they'd be driving her home that night so she didn't have to.

Well, Cris and Landry would drive her. Landry decreed Tilly would remain behind.

Which pissed Tilly off, but she finally accepted.

Landry actually drove Abbey's car for her, after he and Cris helped her ease into the passenger seat. "Our offer is sincere," Landry told her as they drove toward her house. "It won't be an imposition having you there. You already know our secrets," he added with a playful smile. "Although I can't promise you might not need noise-canceling headphones from time to time at night."

She'd been friends with the triad for a couple of years and already knew all about their dynamic. "No problem there."

"We won't upset George, will we?" he joked.

"No, he pretty much puts up with anything. If he doesn't like something, he buries himself in his house, covers himself up, and pulls his head and legs in." She let out a wistful sigh. "Wish I could do that."

"I'm sorry you're having to face this additional stress right now."

"Thanks. You have no idea how much I appreciate all of this. I know it's a burden—"

"Stop. You're like family. If you honestly think we're going to let you deal with this alone, you're mistaken."

"Thank you. I think I'm going to be saying that a lot in the near future."

"You're more than welcome."

She thought they were just going to leave her there at the house once they arrived, but they surprised her yet again by asking to go inside with her.

"We want to see what we're going to need for the move," Cris said, sharing a glance with Landry that didn't fool Abbey for a second.

"Guys, you can't beat him up."

"We weren't going to beat him up," Landry assured her. "But if he happens to cross our paths while we're there, we will suggest to him that it might be a good thing if he makes himself scarce this weekend."

"I should make him do the moving. He said he would."

"I'd prefer to have you settled sooner rather than later," Landry said. "You're not fooling me. Believe me, as someone who's been through enough health issues in their life, I can spot the signs. You can barely function. If we hadn't been home, there's a good chance you wouldn't have been able to get out of your car on your own."

Her face reddened. "Okay," she quietly said.

"Excellent." Landry hooked his arm through hers and matched her slow pace up the front walk while Cris followed behind and carried her purse for her. She wasn't sure who was more startled, Tom or her, when he opened the door and spotted the two men with her.

He quickly backed up a couple of steps, giving the men plenty of room and obviously staying out of their reach.

"Are you all right, Ab?" Tom asked.

"No, she's not fucking all right," Cris snapped. "Are you that stupid?"

"Cris," Landry warned. "Don't make me send you outside."

Abbey felt a little satisfaction that Tom reddened in the face over Cris' comments.

"Let's start with your bedroom," Landry said, leading the way.

The triad, as well as other friends, had been to Abbey's house countless times for dinners and parties, both vanilla and kinky, and knew their way around.

The furniture in the master bedroom was hers. When she'd moved in, they'd put Tom's stuff in the guest room since her set was larger and the bed more comfortable.

She had a desk, filing cabinet, office chair, and bookshelf in the third bedroom that was their home office. Some of the living room furniture was hers, a recliner and some bookshelves, the dinette set, things like that. The large appliances stayed with the house. Then they walked out onto the back lanai. She pointed to a blue plastic kiddie pool leaning against the wall in the corner.

"That's George's inside enclosure. I'll need to transplant his plants from his outside enclosure into it so they don't die. We can take his outside enclosure apart. It's held together with bolts and brackets. I can store it that way."

"We'll take care of that for you," Cris assured her.

"Do you think his pool will fit in your guest room?" she asked.

"Yep," Cris said, kneeling down to study George. The tortoise hadn't dug in for the evening yet, moving toward them at the sound of their voices. "Hey, that's neat how he comes over like that."

"How old is he?" Landry asked. "I must admit I never paid him much attention on our other visits."

"Twenty-one. Drinking age." She forced a laugh.

Tom had joined them on the lanai. She'd tried to ignore him, the way he stood there looking guilty, his hands jammed deep into the pockets of his shorts. "What's going on, Ab?" he finally asked.

Landry took over. "Abbey is moving in with us, at least until after she's fully recovered from her surgery." Landry turned toward Tom.

Despite a good six feet separating them, she didn't miss how Tom stepped back under the weight of the older Dom's glare.

"Your services moving her won't be required," Landry said. "We'll be taking care of it this weekend. Starting on Saturday night and going into Sunday. Oh, and I'm sorry to hear you won't be attending the collaring ceremony after all."

Tom didn't need clarification. He nervously nodded. "Yeah, pass my apologies to Mallory and Askel, please."

Well, they had been more Abbey's friends than Tom's, anyway. She'd been going to Venture for several years before Tom had ever set foot in the place.

Cris stood and walked over to stand next to Landry. He crossed his arms over his chest. "I know the shit about people in glass houses and all that. I know I've made mistakes in the past, but I've had a chance to right them, fortunately. Somehow, I don't think you're ever going to get a chance to make this right."

Tom puffed up, frowning. "Look, I don't owe either of you any explanations. And you're right, Cris. I know the story of how you up and left Tilly. At least I'm man enough to tell Abbey to her face instead of writing her a note and just disappearing without her having a chance to get an explanation."

"That's enough," Landry said. "Nobody's perfect. And you're wrong about something, Tom. Cris left Tilly because he thought I was dying. He owed me nothing. He could have turned his back on me without a second thought and gone back to Tilly without her ever knowing about me or our past together. He made the hard choice. Tilly has forgiven him for it and moved on. Tilly, in fact, made the hard choice by allowing me and Cris into her life after she'd rebuilt hers. She easily could have told me to go fuck myself when I walked into her life and exposed the full truth about what happened and why Cris left. You're making the easy choice, to abandon someone when they need you the most. I just hope one day you can forgive yourself, because you'll find very little sympathy among any of us."

Abbey held her breath, wondering if Tom would dare go up against either man. Yes, Cris was Landry's slave. And yes, Cris now had a quasi-switchy sort of fluid dynamic with Tilly, not really her Master, but not her slave, either. But he had been her Master, and he was a formidable man in his own right.

He was also a martial arts expert.

Tom folded like a wet paper bag. Without a word, he opened the sliders into the house and stepped inside, closing them again behind him.

"Chickenshit," Cris muttered.

Landry turned to Abbey and gently hugged her. "Will you be all right with him tonight? I can run home and get an overnight bag and leave Cris here to wait with you while I do."

"No, I'll be okay. He's not abusive."

She stared at the sliding glass doors, where the vertical blinds still swayed slightly from him having gone inside.

"He's just an asshole," she sadly added. "Problem is, I didn't see how much of an asshole he is until today."

Chapter Five

When John had left work early on Thursday, he'd told his boss that he wasn't sure if he'd be in or not Friday. That he'd have to check on Nancy first, see if she needed him, and play things by ear.

He called her a little after eight that morning. Matt answered the phone and asked if John wouldn't mind coming by since no one else was there yet besides his aunt and uncle. His mom was still asleep but he expected her up any time.

John stopped by a Publix on the way and picked up breakfast foods from their bakery, donuts, pastries, and a couple of bottles of different kinds of juice. He added coffee and coffee fixings to that, knowing their supplies were probably depleted following the onslaught of visitors the day before.

When he arrived, there were only two unfamiliar cars parked in the driveway. Matt met him at the door, reaching for some of the grocery bags.

"Thanks for coming back."

"Of course. I'm sorry I can't do more than just help."

He couldn't *fix* this, or even make it right. Nothing he could do could *fix* this, and fixing things wasn't just in his nature, it was his *job*. He *fixed* things so people were safe at work. When problems occurred, he fixed them, or made sure they got fixed, and took measures to make sure that, barring human error or mechanical failure, they didn't happen again.

Not being able to fix something frustrated him to no end and didn't help him at all with processing his grief.

He ended up staying until just after noon, when other friends and extended family returned to the house. After going out and getting sandwich platters to help feed everyone, he quietly said his good-byes before slipping out and returning home.

Drained.

Numb.

And this is how it starts.

He called work and told them that, no, he wouldn't be in today, but they could call him if they needed him. After clearing out his e-mail via his work phone, he changed into shorts and went out into the backyard to weed and mow. The sun beat down on his bare back as he worked and tried to avoid his thoughts and keep his head clear and focused on the task at hand.

After several hours of that, he took a dip in the pool to rinse the sweat off and then returned to the house. Naked, his usual preferred state when home alone, he started cleaning, even though it really didn't need it. Living room first, ceiling to floor, dusting every square inch of surface and knickknacks, moving every piece of furniture even though he could easily get under stuff with a dust mop, thanks to the faux wood laminate floors he had.

From there to the dining room, the foyer, and his bedroom. By nine o'clock that night, he'd cleaned all three bathrooms, the powder room, and started on the kitchen, including emptying the fridge and scrubbing it from freezer to base, inside and out, and he was caught up on his laundry.

By midnight, he'd worn himself to exhaustion. There wasn't much different about the house, because his usual cleaning routine rotated him through all the rooms at least once a week, but he'd achieved his main goal.

He'd managed to drive thoughts out of his head, replaced by whatever task was at hand.

After another large rum and Coke in the hot tub, he collapsed into bed, setting his alarm for six the next morning.

If he timed it right, he'd have enough time to wash and vacuum his car before he had to get ready for the funeral.

*　*　*　*

John arrived at the funeral home an hour early Saturday morning, suspecting Nancy and the kids would already be there, and that the place would likely be packed by the time for the service. He parked a couple of blocks away so it'd be easier to get out after the service and head over to Venture. Depending on how long the memorial service lasted, he would probably make it to the club in time to witness the collaring.

He didn't want to miss it. Askel and Mallory were a cute couple. He liked both of them, even though he'd known Askel longer. He'd even let Askel use him as a model—while fully hooded and completely unrecognizable, of course—for a couple of photo shoots.

No one knew that besides Askel. John hadn't wanted it publicized.

When Askel had called John yesterday morning to confirm he'd be there and asking him to tone down his usual shtick because of Tilly's already stressed mental state, he'd been happy to agree. John didn't pry, but Askel mentioned something about a friend of Tilly's going through a rough patch and already being nearly murderous over it.

Whether Tilly knew it or not, John liked her. Not just because it was fun to push her buttons, but because he knew how fiercely dedicated she was to her friends. He hadn't officially played with her before, although he'd been the willing recipient of her ire at a few collarings.

A somber funeral home employee led John back to a room where Nancy, her kids, and some of her other family were waiting for things to be finalized in the largest room where the service would be held.

She stood and gave him a tearful smile, hugging him. "Thank you for coming, John. I really appreciate you being here."

"I wish I had something to say that would make this better. I don't have anything except I'm sorry, and if you need anything, you can always call me, day or night."

"I know. And I appreciate it. I'm still…in shock."

"I can imagine."

Another family member entered, diverting Nancy's attention and allowing John to quietly step around some of the others to where Matt and Paul sat flanking Emma. The poor girl looked like she was in shock, too.

He couldn't blame her.

He gave them all hugs before melting back along the wall, slowly making his way over to a counter where a coffee machine, iced bottles of water, and some light snacks had been set out.

He knew why. Things relatives and friends could easily push onto the most grief-stricken of relatives, to keep their blood sugar from dropping and having them faint during the stressful time ahead of them.

Unfortunately, John was all too familiar with this funeral home. He'd attended funerals here before.

The last one being Kaden's a couple of years earlier.

Irony.

That he'd be attending his best friend's funeral and then leaving straight for Venture, when the last funeral he'd attended here had been for a friend in the lifestyle, met through Venture.

Although then, as today, everyone had been dressed vanilla. The only difference then was that he knew the significance of the necklaces and bracelets some of the attendees wore.

Distracting himself with the *Are They Kinky or Not* game wouldn't be possible today. As far as he knew, Mick and Nancy had been vanilla. Or, if they were kinky, it hadn't been something Mick had ever discussed with John. John had never crossed paths with them via Venture or the Suncoast Society munches or private parties, either.

Today would be an endurance test. A mental strength test.

To see how well he could wear the "normal" mask and hold himself together around people who had no idea what went on in that extremely compartmentalized section of his life. The one he kept well-hidden from everyone else.

Something not even Mick had known about, and Mick knew the worst about him.

The only one who'd known the worst about him who'd still been alive. The only person who really mattered in his life anymore.

The only person left who'd metaphorically given him kicks in the ass when he started to delve too deeply into his own belly button to the exclusion of living life.

Maybe Mick was right. Maybe I need to get another dog.

His last one, Pepper, had died of cancer four years ago. He'd resisted getting another one, his heart still not fully healed from having her put to sleep when her pain and condition had reached an inevitable point where it was crueler to force her keep living just so he didn't have to grieve than to do the humane thing. She'd been sixteen, definitely a long and full life, but even more grief for him as he tried to adjust to that final decision.

He'd held her in his lap as the vet gave her the shot, whispering what a good dog she was and how much he loved her, getting one last weak tail thump from her before she'd left him for good.

Now, her ashes rested in an ornate carved box on his living room shelf, next to a picture of her, and her collar.

As the small room began to fill with more extended family and Nancy's close friends, John edged his way out and walked into the main room, where the service would be held. He picked up a program from a stack of them on a table by the main doorway before he took a seat in a pew a few rows back from the front, behind the section roped off as reserved for family.

Despite his friendship with Mick, he'd never presume to insert himself that way and sit up there unless Nancy or the kids asked him.

Besides, this way he could leave after the ceremony ended without having to explain where he was going or why. Actually, to outright lie where he was going and why he had to leave. He knew everyone was going back to Nancy's for a wake later. He suspected his absence wouldn't be missed.

And going to a collaring, an upbeat affirmation of life, would be a welcomed relief for him, even if all he did was sit and watch and didn't speak to a single person while he was there.

I wonder how many people will even recognize me dressed like this?

Probably not many. A few of the long-time regulars, maybe.

Someone had put together a slideshow of Mick's life, from childhood to present, which started playing on a screen at the front of the room. John wistfully smiled when he spotted himself in a few of them. Good times, smiles filling the pictures.

People started filtering in for the service, taking their seats. Then family escorted Nancy and the kids in about thirty minutes before the start time.

The service painfully demanded entry through his mental walls, pounding on them, wanting access. Wanting to release the growing pressure inside those hermetically sealed compartments where he was desperately trying to contain his emotions, to cool the glowing lava. He tuned out as much of it as he could, knowing if he let it seep in too deeply he'd lose it there in a room full of mostly strangers.

When the service finally ended about an hour later, he managed to slip through a side door after Nancy and the kids had been ushered out first. Loosening his tie, he pulled off his suit jacket and carried it as he quickly walked through the growing heat to his car. Inside, with the engine running and the AC going full-blast, he struggled to empty his mind and failed.

Too many things. Not regrets, exactly. Realities.

What am I really *doing with my life?*

He'd hit a point of stasis. Coasting along and gradually digging himself a rut as he rounded the track time and time again. Not an unpleasant rut, to be sure, but had he really fulfilled his potential?

Maybe it's time to try to enter the dating pool again.

That was a joke. The last relationship he'd had, when he'd tried to broach the subject of BDSM, she'd freaked out and ended things with him before he'd even gotten to the point of explaining he wanted her to be his Top, not the other way around.

Tony and the others were always counseling newbies to fish in the right pond.

Hell, lately he hadn't even been dipping his hook in the water. His proverbial fishing rod lay gathering dust in a locked and abandoned closet somewhere. Sure he could find play partners at the club without any trouble. That only went so far, filled only one aspect of his emptiness.

Yet he wasn't sure he needed a relationship, either. Wanted one, sure. Who didn't?

I really am a masochist, going to a collaring. Especially on the heels of a funeral.

John still had more than half of the bottle of rum left. When he finally left the club that night, he could go home, pour another stiff drink, and think about scrubbing down the garage, even though it didn't need it.

Busy work.

If I can't be happy, at least I can be productive.

Chapter Six

Fortunately, Tom voluntarily slept in the guest room Thursday night. Abbey didn't even have to ask him, which was a relief.

It was a battle she'd dreaded, and she didn't think she should have to give up her bed due to his asshattery.

He didn't emerge from his room before she left for work on Friday morning, either, although he'd started the coffeepot before she got up. On her way home from work early Friday afternoon, she stopped by a storage place that sold moving supplies and loaded her car with boxes, packing tape, bubble wrap, markers, and other things she'd need.

When she arrived home, Tom wasn't there, but he returned a little while later with groceries.

"How much is my share?" she tonelessly asked.

"Don't worry about it." He set about putting things away while she retreated to her room to take a hot shower and lie down. He knocked on her door a little after six that evening. "Dinner's ready."

They ate watching the evening news, no conversation as she sat on the sofa and he occupied the recliner.

It felt painfully uncomfortable in a way even the agony in her back did not.

He retreated to his bedroom after cleaning up the dishes.

The next morning, Tom left the house early, with his luggage packed, and said he'd stay at a hotel in Tampa until his flight out Monday morning.

Fine with her. It meant less contact with him.

Later Saturday morning, it was actually Landry and Cris who

picked up Abbey, because Tilly needed to assist with the preparations at the club and help Mallory get ready. Tilly had bought Abbey a present and sent it with her men, though. The pink tiger-print cane was adjustable, and Cris was careful to make sure it was the right height for her.

"Tilly said if she sees you not using it today," Landry said, "once you're healed up, she reserves the right to spank you."

She struggled not to cry, didn't want to cry today. Today was supposed to be a celebration for their friends, not a day for her to throw herself a pity party.

The two men took her out for a late brunch, then back to their house so she could change before they headed to the club. Abbey couldn't help but feel guilty that she wasn't at the club and helping. Usually, she pitched in when someone had a collaring or wedding at the club, helping get the chairs set up and the decorations placed.

Once they arrived at Venture, Landry got Abbey settled on one of the sofas and made sure she was comfortable before he and Cris went to see if their help was needed. It was still early, and the bulk of the expected crowd hadn't arrived yet.

She felt more than a little useless just sitting there, but her pain was worse than normal. Trying to help, knowing what her day would be like tomorrow with the impending move, would be stupid.

The door from the outer lobby opened and a man who looked vaguely familiar walked in. He scanned the room, apparently searching for someone, before his gaze settled on her. He looked handsome, brown hair and greenish hazel eyes, and dressed in a nice suit and tie. Though he wore a rather somber expression.

It was only when he walked over to her that she realized who he was.

"Gilo!" she softly hissed. "Are you *crazy*? Tilly will *kill* you if she sees you here."

He sadly smiled, indicating the sofa. "May I sit?"

A switch flipped inside her, sensing something drastically

different about the man today. "Yeah. What's wrong? What happened?"

He slowly lowered himself onto the couch, as if weighed down by an invisible burden. "Just came from the funeral for my oldest friend."

Abbey felt horrible for the man. "Oh, dammit. I'm so sorry, John."

"Yeah." He seemed to study his feet for a moment. "Sudden. Drives home how short life is. Don't worry, Askel called me yesterday and asked me to keep it toned down today. Frankly, I don't feel like acting out anyway. But I didn't want to miss their ceremony. I came straight here from there." He flapped his tie a little. "Hence the monkey suit."

She rested a hand on his shoulder. "I'm so, so sorry." Actually, she sort of liked this look on him. Then again, a well-tailored suit on a man was one of her personal fetishes.

"Thanks." He took a deep breath and let it out again. "Was not expecting this."

"What happened? Or would you rather not talk about it?"

"Shit happened. Complications from a routine colonoscopy. He was dead twenty-four hours later."

She'd played with Gilo a couple of times years ago, before she'd met Tom and started a relationship with him. They hadn't had much contact outside the club, and she wasn't even sure what he did for a living. The only reason she knew his real name was because when she played with someone, that was a requirement for her in case something went wrong. Even if only playing at the club.

"Jesus."

"Yeah." He forced a smile and looked at her. "So what's new in your world?" He nodded toward the cane. "I've never seen you with that before."

"I thought you'd heard. Ruined my back. And my relationship's in the shitter." Before she knew it, just sitting there with him, alone like that, the story spilled out of her.

"Holy crap, Abbey. That sucks. What an asshole. I'm sorry, but that's just wrong. Especially if you're having surgery."

At that point, Tilly appeared with Mallory and Chelbie in tow, but they headed straight for the bathroom changing area without so much as a glance their way.

She noticed John froze, carefully watching Tilly, only relaxing once she and the two younger women were in the bathroom.

"Hey, how about I make you a deal," Abbey said, laying a hand on his arm.

He returned his focus to her. "Yeah?"

She forced a smile she didn't really feel. "How about you let me hang off your arm and help me hobble around today for the ceremony, and I'll protect you from Tilly." She was only half joking.

"Thanks, I appreciate it. But I'd help you hobble around even if you don't want to protect me. Some of us are still gentlemen, even if Tom isn't."

As they sat and talked, she realized there was so much about the man she didn't know, that he was an engineer, that he was intelligent and funny and definitely far more than just the smart-assed masochistic clown many of the club members saw him portray.

"Can I ask you something?" she said.

"Sure."

"Why the SAM act?"

He smiled. "Stress relief. As you can imagine, my job is pretty stressful. This is how I process that stress."

"By getting it beaten out of you?"

"Yeah, I know. Look, this might sound out of the blue, and no is a totally fine answer, but I've got a four-bedroom house I'm rattling around in. If you want, you can move in with me. I'm only ten minutes from Tilly's place. After your surgery, she can still come over and help you out while I'm at work."

She stared at him. "What?"

"Yeah. I own my house. My last roommate moved out over a year ago. Only reason he lived with me was he'd lost his job and needed time to get back on his feet. In fact, the room he was using, I just have a few boxes stored in it. I can have it cleared out in under an hour."

* * * *

John didn't know why he suddenly made the offer. In fact, as soon as he did, he mentally kicked himself, knowing that it probably made him look like a douche or a desperate idiot or something.

But the pain in her expression, the ocean of sadness in her green eyes as she recounted what Tom had done and the cold, clinical way the man had justified his actions to her, it viscerally pissed John off to the depths of his being.

Abbey was a good woman. She deserved to be treated better than that. Even if just as friends, he wanted to offer her the help. Yes, he tended to stay on the fringes of their social group, afraid the visibility of his job might make him vulnerable to being outed if he ran into anyone he worked with. That was why he usually wore a hood or at least a mask when playing at the club. He'd long regretted not becoming closer to her sooner, when they'd played before.

Instead of shooting him down like he thought she would, she said the weirdest thing. "I have a tortoise. Is that going to be a problem?"

Confused, he stared at her. "I don't know what that means."

"Huh?"

"Okay, back up. My hearing's not that great. What did you say you have?"

"A tortoise. You know, like a turtle, but not. He's my pet."

I. Am. An. Idiot.

He felt blood fill his face. "Ah, okay. Sorry. Now I'm tracking. No, that's not a problem."

"I've got an indoor enclosure for him I can put him in. I'm going to have to break down his outdoor one. I have it on a screened lanai right now."

"You could set it up on my lanai. I've got a pool and everything."

"They don't swim."

"Oh. Well, then I guess we'll keep the kid-proof screen up around the pool."

She smiled and tucked a stray strand of her reddish-auburn hair behind her ear. For the first time that day, his soul felt a little lighter. He'd actually made someone smile.

"You say that like I've said yes."

"I'm an optimist." He returned to serious mode. "Look, just friends, no pressure, no nothing. I've even got a roommate lease you can sign if you want to make things legal. Although I might have to add a clause prohibiting Tilly from killing me. And if you say no, at least let me help you with the move tomorrow, please?"

She actually laughed a little. "Might take more than a clause to prevent Tilly from killing you. Why do you bait her, anyway?"

He shrugged. "People laugh. It's fun knowing I can push her buttons like that. If someone specifically pulls me aside beforehand and asks me not to goof around, like today, then I don't. But people love watching her get riled up. I like making people laugh."

"And you're a masochist."

"There is that," he agreed. "She kicks a mean stiletto heel."

"So isn't that kind of nonconsensually pulling her into your kink?"

He considered that. "Hadn't really thought about it like that. Actually, I guess you have a very valid point."

"Takes a big man to admit when he's wrong."

"I never have a problem admitting when I'm wrong. Although I frequently question myself when I'm right."

A few minutes later, as more people started gathering for the ceremony, John offered his seat on the sofa to a woman who was a friend of Abbey's. Before he stood, however, Abbey reached for his arm.

"Hey, are you busy after this?" she asked.

"No. I was just going to go home and drown my sorrows in a tub of Chunky Monkey."

She offered him a smile. "Would you mind if I went with you? To look at your place? I don't want to say yes or no until we've had a chance to talk more. And if you don't mind taking me home, I'd like you to meet George."

"George?"

"My tortoise."

"Okay." He paused, thinking. "How about we go to my place, then dinner—my treat—and then I'll take you home."

She smiled. "You have yourself a deal."

He stood, remaining close so he could help Abbey when it came time to move over to the chairs for the ceremony. He wasn't paying attention when Tilly emerged from the bathroom with Mallory and Chelbie.

It was only when Tilly did a double-take and backed up to look at him that he realized how vulnerable he was.

Thunderclouds filled Tilly's face. "What the *hell* are you doing here?"

He held up his hands to placate her. "Calm down, Tilly," he said. "I just came from a funeral. Don't worry, I'm not going to cause trouble." He faced Mallory and gave her a slight, respectful bow. "Congratulations. You look beautiful. I hope you and Kel have many years of happiness together."

Mallory looked a little shocked at first, like maybe she didn't recognize him in street clothes.

He was beyond amused at how Tilly's jaw opened and closed a couple of times, like she was going to say something but had been rendered speechless. Finally, she jabbed a finger in his face. "Behave yourself, or you won't walk straight ever again."

He cocked his head, arching an eyebrow at her. He didn't want to get into it with her then, and didn't feel like explaining himself. "Believe it or not, I do have boundaries. You don't give me credit for all the times I haven't said a peep during a ceremony simply because I was asked ahead of time not to."

Tilly let out something resembling a snarl. "Yeah? Well...I'm going to have my eye on you, buster."

He blew her a kiss. "I'm flattered." He flashed her a playful smile.

Tilly let out one final snort and stormed away, Ross giving John a silent laugh and shake of his head as he led Mallory toward the other side of the play space where the chairs had been set up.

He turned to Abbey. "I think it's time." He stepped in to help her stand, keeping his right arm around her waist and offering his left for her to hold on to as he helped her across the room.

Abbey playfully *tsked*. "You just couldn't help yourself, could you?"

He shrugged. "I was good. I behaved myself."

As he glanced around, he caught sight of Tilly glaring at him. She pointed at her own eyes with two fingers on her right hand, then at him, and back to herself.

I've got my eyes on you.

He blew Tilly another silent kiss. Then he helped Abbey ease down into her seat before taking the one next to her.

Abbey gently poked him in the ribs and mouthed *Behave* at him.

But she was smiling.

And, he noticed, she kept her arm hooked through his. Whether for her own comfort, or because she still thought he might act up, he didn't know.

Considering it'd been over five years since he'd gotten laid, he wouldn't question the gesture. It felt good to have some gentle human contact that didn't involve pain, or comforting someone in their grief, even though he enjoyed pain. Just in a different way.

It was nice to have a little normalcy for a change.

Yes, he'd behave himself today. Because the last thing he felt like was acting like a fool.

But mostly because Kel had asked him not to.

Still, he wouldn't deny it felt good getting under Tilly's skin.

I owe her an apology before we leave. If she doesn't kill me when she finds out what Abbey's thinking about doing.

And he wasn't sure that Tilly might not do just that.

It was hard to miss the frequent glares Tilly sent his way throughout the brief ceremony. Only when Tilly was distracted because she was taking pictures for Kel during Mallory's piercing did Tilly's attention waver from him.

Abbey leaned in. "I might be able to trip her with my cane to give you a running start," she softly joked. "But that's all I've got."

He had to press his lips together to keep from laughing out loud and drawing Tilly's attention as well as her ire. "No, hopefully Cris and Landry will run interference." All joking aside, he knew what a dedicated friend Tilly was to those she considered "adopted" into her family.

He respected her for it, even if Tilly didn't know that. A lot of people respected her, even if in public they joked about their fear of her. She'd helped mentor plenty of newbie women, who'd been kept safe from jackass predators in the BDSM lifestyle simply because they had Tilly as their "protector."

He also knew she'd been through a lot in her life, especially the last several turbulent years after Landry came into her life, bringing Cris back into it as well.

Yeah, that had been a shock to the entire local community who knew the history there.

John had been one of the first to privately welcome Cris back, albeit with the warning that if he fucked up again, John would be one of the first in line to string him up by his balls.

Fortunately, Tilly, Landry, and Cris seemed to have formed a triad that worked for all three of them.

When the ceremony ended, John remained in his seat because Abbey made no move to stand. Eventually Tilly, closely followed by Landry and Cris, made her way over.

"What's going on?" Tilly asked, her murderous glare now toned back to assault with intent.

"You have to promise not to get upset," Abbey said.

"I make no such promise. *Especially* when it's prefaced by that warning."

"Tilly," Landry said. "Hear her out."

"John's offered to let me move in with him—"

"Oh, *fuck* no—"

"Tilly," Landry and Cris both said.

John took over. "I have a huge house and plenty of room, and I'm only ten minutes from your place. You can still help her out after her surgery. If Abbey even says yes. She hasn't yet. I'm going to take her over there now to look at it, then I'm taking her out to dinner. I'll bring her home after."

Tilly looked like she was about to explode.

Landry, smooth-talking ex-pat Frenchman that he was, laid a staying hand on Tilly's arm. "How about this," he said. "We're no longer required here tonight. We'll say our good-byes and follow you to your house. Then all of us can go out to dinner."

"That sounds like a plan to me," John agreed.

"Are you *shitting* me?" Tilly asked Landry. "You're okay with her maybe moving in with this guy?"

"Love, your concern for your friend is admirable. However, she is an adult. Our offer still stands, and it's not yet confirmed she will move in with him. Let us not lose our composure over this, hmm?"

This was worth it to watch Tilly trying to keep her head from exploding. Finally, she threw her hands up in disgust and stormed off toward the bathroom, presumably to change into street clothes.

Landry and Cris watched her go, the men wearing nearly identical smirks.

"You have your hands full with her, don't you?" John asked.

"You have no idea," Landry said, a smile slipping across his lips. "But she's worth every bit of it."

"Do you think she's going to be pissed off at me?" Abbey asked.

"No," Cris said. "She's just having trouble wrapping her head around the fact that John has a life and identity outside of Venture."

"Our sweet Tilly is a vicious, sadistic thing," Landry said. "Especially when she gets an idea in her head and goes into tenaciously protective mode."

"Yeah, I'll work it out with her," John said. "I will admit it's been pointed out to me that even though one of my kinks is making people laugh by making Tilly blow up, it wasn't fair of me to do that without her being in on it."

"Hey, better you than me," Cris said. "I know she packs a wallop. I think I still have bruises from a couple of years ago when she let me have it."

"Ah, but you deserved it," Landry said.

Cris shrugged. "Never said I didn't. It was worth taking every last one of them to get her to trust me again."

Landry slung an arm around his shoulders and pulled him close, kissing him on the temple. "And you have no idea how glad I am that she has."

John felt a slightly envious pang tweak his heart. No, he wasn't gay, or bi, but the love the two men shared not just for each other, but for Tilly as well, was palpable.

Don't even go there.

His offer to Abbey was genuine, and without any strings attached.

If it meant he could help her out, great. If one day, maybe, she wanted more from him…

Well, he wouldn't deny that would be nice, too.

Until then, he'd keep his cock locked up tight and his emotions in check. She'd been through enough lately, and the last thing she needed was to feel pressure from him.

Although he wouldn't mind taking a whack or two at Tom himself.

Chapter Seven

Abbey didn't understand why it felt so comfortable clinging to John's arm, but she wouldn't question it.

For the first time in two months, despite the odd looks she got from a couple of people who were probably wondering why she seemed to be there with John and not Tom, she almost felt…

Normal.

Since she'd hurt her back, she'd only been to the club twice. Mostly because Tom had insisted it'd be good for her to go. She certainly hadn't felt like going, and hadn't been able to do much more than sit and talk with friends.

She wasn't so dense she missed the disappointment in his expression, in his voice, when she wouldn't play with him.

He didn't come right out and say it, but the fact that he'd packed a small toy bag each time and brought it showed her more than any words. He thought he'd hidden it from her in the trunk, but she'd heard him putting it together each time and taking it out to the car. He never brought it into the club, but he'd kept steering the conversations that direction, like he was hinting around that he'd like to play.

He always did think he was smarter than me.

If he'd simply asked if he could play with someone else, she would have said yes, but she wasn't going to reward his passive-aggressive behavior by jumping ahead like that.

Yet, he'd rebuffed her efforts to help him out sexually after she'd gotten hurt. She didn't understand it.

Not that it matters now, I guess.

It still grated at her that she'd never put all that together before now. And it hurt that he'd said he loved her, yet when she'd really needed him the most, he ran away.

Grieving that loss would have to come later. Shoving her feelings for Tom into a closet and locking the door was the only way she could get through the next few days and weeks. Once she'd healed up and was back on her feet—and alone in her own place—only then would she allow herself to grieve.

John slowly matched her pace as he walked her out to his car, Tilly following and sheepdogging Landry and Cris in front of her. Before John helped Abbey into the car, she turned to Tilly.

"He's not an ax murderer."

"I hope not."

However, if looks could kill, Tilly would have murdered John a thousand times over.

Just in the past five minutes.

"Give him a chance."

"I've given him plenty of chances and he acts like an asshole."

"I'm standing *right* here," John lightly said.

Tilly reached out and poked him in the arm. "Yeah? Well, I'm right *here*. I'm warning you, you hurt her, and there won't be anywhere for you to run where you'll be safe."

"I believe you," he said. Abbey gave John full credit, he didn't even flinch in front of Tilly's onslaught of thermonuclear hatred.

In fact, besides the obvious, there seemed to be something…different about John today. Not just his fresh grief, either.

Something…

Strong.

Or maybe it was just she felt tired and in a lot of pain and what was that line about the kindness of strangers?

Although John wasn't a total stranger. They weren't exactly friends, but they were acquaintances.

Even though she knew the area his house was in, she wasn't

prepared for it to be so...

Normal.

I'm doing a lot of thinking in ellipses today.

What's up with that?

The subdivision was a couple of years older than Tilly's, the lots a little larger, the trees a little taller. The lawns were manicured, apparently an HOA mandate based on how uniform they all looked.

Tilly, riding with Landry, and Cris following in Tilly's SUV, pulled up in the driveway as John was helping Abbey out of the car.

As John walked her up to the front door, he waited until Abbey was steady and using her cane before he unlocked the door.

Then he turned to Tilly. "Wait just a minute while I go hide the bodies."

She frowned. "What?"

Abbey couldn't help but giggle at his playfully evil grin. "I need to shut the alarm off," he said. "Give me a second."

"Well, why didn't you say *that*?"

Abbey hooked her free arm through Tilly's. "Cut him some slack."

"You sound like you've made up your mind."

"I haven't yet, but please, he's being nice."

"Still right here," he said as he opened the door and entered the foyer. A few seconds later, they heard the distinctive sound of a keypad being punched before another beep.

"Okay, all clear." He flipped on a light and Tilly helped her inside.

Abbey's first impression was that John was a better housekeeper than she and Tom were. Her house was always presentable, and tidy, and clean. But especially since her fall, it certainly wasn't to the standards she wished it was.

John's standards, even when he wasn't expecting company, were obviously higher.

Not even a museum feel. Just...squeaky clean.

John walked through another doorway. "Feel free to search it top to bottom," John called out to Tilly.

"Cris," Landry drawled as he looked around. "You've been slacking."

"When someone doesn't have much of a life, they tend to express themselves in other ways," John said. "Anyone want anything to drink or snack on before dinner?"

Tilly led Abbey toward John's voice. The place had a homey feel, comfortable. He obviously wasn't a pig. Her quick eye did spot a half-full pot of coffee, now cold, sitting in the coffeemaker.

She heard Tilly click her tongue against the roof of her mouth as she craned her head around, trying to find…something.

Damned ellipses.

"Well?" Abbey asked Tilly.

"I haven't seen his bathrooms yet. He could be a complete and total pig."

Landry let out a snort. "Love, I think you're grasping at straws."

The kitchen was actually nicer than the one at her house. Abbey missed cooking. It was a chore she never minded, because she loved cooking and baking. It would be a joy to roll out dough on the large granite counter tops.

Now, it was all she could do to lift a plate, much less lift a pot or pan full of hot food or boiling water.

"This is beautiful, John," Abbey said.

"Thank you. It's home."

He gave them the full tour, Abbey fully conscious that he kept his steps slow, pacing himself to Abbey.

It was considerate.

Tom would walk and then stop and impatiently wait for her, unless she specifically asked to hold his arm because of her pain.

The bedroom that would be hers, if she wanted it, was actually larger than the one at Tilly's house. She'd have her own en suite bathroom, too. By the time they returned to the dining room, even

Tilly looked like she had to grudgingly admit it was nice. Tilly helped her down to the couch.

"What about a lease?" Tilly asked.

Landry interceded again. "Love, let me handle the contracts."

"I can print you off the one my last roommate signed," John said.

"How many roommates have you had?" Tilly asked, her tone finally edging away from confrontational.

"Before him, two others. Similar situations, people needing a place to stay to get their life together."

"Kind of like me," Abbey quietly said.

"I'm sorry," John said. "I didn't mean it like that."

"It's the truth." She looked around the beautiful house, a house nicer than the one she currently lived in. The pool was gorgeous, and he even had a hot tub. "How much a month in rent?"

"I'm fully cognizant of workman's comp issues. How much can you afford without it putting a serious strain on you?"

"Well, right now, my share of the rent and utilities is around nine hundred a month, depending on the light and water bill. But we don't have a pool."

"I'm not going to charge you that much. My friend only paid a hundred a month, plus groceries."

"I have to pay you more than that."

"Then you tell me what you want to pay."

She sucked at money negotiations. Tie someone up—or down—and beat their ass? No problem negotiating *that*.

Money issues, however, she hated with a passion.

"I want to be fair."

"Well, you tell me what you can afford."

Tilly held up her hands. "This will go on all night if I don't step in. John, is three hundred a month all right? Plus groceries?"

"Sure."

Tilly looked at Abbey. "Will that work for you?"

"Yeah. It'll actually help me out a lot."

"Settled. Shake on it."

John laughed. "You haven't given me a full-body cavity search yet, Tilly. Sure you don't want to dig up my backyard?"

Tilly let out an exhausted-sounding sigh. "John," she said, "I can tell she's already made up her mind." She turned to Abbey. "Look, I'll drop my objections to this if you promise me that if it doesn't work out, you'll tell me immediately and let me move you in with us. Okay?"

"How about this," John said. "I'll print the contract out and we'll take it to dinner and go over it there. If you want any changes to it, we'll make them, and then come back here to print and sign it."

"You're sure you don't mind me having George?" Abbey asked.

"I wouldn't have brought you here if I did."

"In the house?"

"In the house."

Tilly let out another exhausted sigh. "He's saying it's okay, honey. Let it go."

"Why do you sound mad at me?" Abbey asked.

"I'm not! Well, I'm mad, but at Tom, not you." She slumped to the couch, next to Abbey. "I know you loved him. For him to just walk away like this, you have to admit it's a massive trigger of the bad kind for me."

"Shit," Cris muttered. "Guess I'm getting beaten tonight."

* * * *

John deliberately went out of his way to not goad Tilly the rest of the evening. For starters, he felt emotionally wrung out. Second, he could tell Tilly was trying to make an effort.

And third, he didn't want to make things any harder on Abbey.

Okay, slide the third reason to the top of the list.

The more he learned about what happened, the angrier he felt at Tom. After Landry went through the contract over dinner and pronounced it satisfactory, they paid their checks and started toward the parking lot.

Tilly sent Abbey ahead with Cris and Landry and held John back to speak to him.

At first, John thought maybe she was going to give him another one of her warnings, but she actually shocked him.

"Thank you," she quietly said.

"No castration threats?"

She rolled her eyes. "Thank you for stepping up to do this for her. I really appreciate it."

"Of course. But you have to promise me one thing."

Doubt flickered across her features. "What?"

He held out his hand to her. "If Tom gets the shit kicked out of him, I get to help. At least I get to help hold him down."

Tilly smiled, genuine, without the snark barrier in place, and shook with him. "Deal."

"You aren't threatening him, are you?" Abbey called back to them.

Tilly hooked her arm through John's. "No," she said. "We've signed a truce." She squeezed his arm, hard, and muttered low enough only he could hear. "For now."

When they returned to John's house, he printed two copies of the contracts for them to both sign. After he did, he handed Abbey a key, and then he handed one to Tilly, too.

"What's this for?" Tilly asked.

"Front door," he said.

"Why are you giving me one?"

"Are you not going to be helping her after her surgery?"

"Yeah?"

"Well, then you'll need a key. That way she won't have to get up to let you in. I'll show you how the alarm pad works and program you a custom code."

Tilly looked at the key he'd given her as if she couldn't believe she was holding it. "You're just *handing* me a key to your house?"

"Yep. And you two are the only other people who have them besides me."

"Huh. I'll be damned."

Abbey smiled over her friend's reaction and it lit John's heart.

Oh, shit. Don't go there.

"Tilly," Abbey said. "You have to admit, he's trying."

"Yeah, yeah." But she smiled. "Why couldn't you have hooked up with him instead of Tom?"

Then Abbey turned the full force of her green gaze on him. "I'm beginning to wonder that myself," she said.

* * * *

Why *hadn't* she hooked up with John before now? They'd played together a few times. Then she'd met Tom, John hadn't been around the club much, and things just naturally progressed from there. She wasn't poly, didn't have the time or energy to manage more than one relationship at a time. Not even multiple play partners, once she had a steady, primary relationship.

What if John had come to the club more often during that time? Would she have ended up with him instead of Tom?

Stop that.

Woulda, coulda, shoulda wouldn't help her through this.

After they finished with the lease contract and finalizing arrangements for the move the next day, John drove her home. She invited him inside to look around, even though Cris and Landry had already given him a basic rundown of what she had to move. He brought her bags inside for her, leaving them on the bed so she wouldn't have to carry them.

"Can I meet George?" he asked.

"Sure."

She led him outside to the lanai. George was, predictably, dug in under a layer of substrate inside his house. "If you lift that off, you'll see him in there."

"I don't want to disturb him." He knelt down and peered in. "I can sort of see him. How big will he get?"

"He's fully grown. He's not like a sulcata."

"A what?"

"Sulcatas get to be a couple hundred pounds. He's about as big as he'll get."

"And he's really over twenty years old?"

"Yep." She lowered herself into one of the chairs on the lanai. "We've been together a long time."

"How long do they live?"

"Fifty years or more, easily."

"Wow. That's cool."

"Yep. But they don't swim. He'll drown if he gets in a pool."

"Then we'll make sure that doesn't happen."

Abbey stared at the tortoise enclosure. "This was his first large outdoor home," she said. "He's been so happy here. Before, I always lived in an apartment. He could run around inside when I was home, but he didn't have a permanent outside home."

"How can you tell he's happy?"

"Oh, when he's awake, he'll come to me. We have a little daily ritual where I feed him romaine lettuce as a snack. He's been able to free graze most of the year in this enclosure." She choked back tears again. "Guess I'm back to buying his food for him and doing some container gardening for his greens."

"I'm sure we can do something for him like that at my place."

"I'm not going to ask you to take care of that. I might need help with his water or something, but I need to do as much as I can. And once I get my own place…" She didn't want to think that far ahead and knew she needed to. "I'll get either a condo or an apartment once I'm on my own. So he's back to indoor living as of tomorrow."

She wanted to get off that topic. "So, tomorrow. Want me to make breakfast?"

He offered her a smile. "Tomorrow morning, I'll be here at seven and I'll bring you breakfast," John said. "Your job tomorrow is to supervise. That's it. We're going to have enough help from everyone that you can sit and watch."

"I feel like I'm putting everyone out."

"Hey, you know how this works. We'll have over a dozen people, it looks like. Askel and Mallory even wanted to help. He texted me earlier when he found out about the move, but we told them no, to enjoy their day together tomorrow."

"Sort of a honeymoon?"

"Yeah. But he did offer free storage space, if you need it, over at his place."

"They're so sweet." She didn't want to mentally steer in that direction, but her thoughts disobeyed her. "It's nice to see a happy ending for someone, even if I don't get one."

"If it's any consolation, look at it like this. It's a fresh start for you. And George." He smiled, playful, encouraging.

He was trying so hard to cheer her up, and she could see that.

She appreciated it more than she had the words to express to him.

"Thank you for all of this."

"Hey, if nothing else, at least you're the reason Tilly won't one day murder me." He grinned, making her laugh.

"True."

He squatted down in front of her. "Tomorrow, please, don't hurt yourself. We know you're in pain, and we know you've been trying to hide that. You will find yourself surrounded by a bunch of Doms ordering you to sit down if you try to do too much. And if anything, we are a group of people used to restraining people, and we won't hesitate to tie you down to keep you from hurting yourself. So let us do it. Okay?"

"Okay." She didn't have any fight in her. Pain had robbed her of most of that, and her emotional agony stole the rest. "When I'm feeling better, can we use your house to have them all over so I can cook them a thank-you dinner?"

"Of course we can." He stood and helped her to her feet and back inside. "So try to get a good night's sleep, and I'll see you in the morning." She saw him out, locking the door behind him.

As she undressed, she looked around. Her last night there, in that house.

She remembered the first night she'd spent there, after moving in with Tom. Wasn't her first night spent at his house, but it had felt like a solid new start. No, marriage was never part of the equation for her, but she'd been in love with him. Loved him. *Thought* he loved her.

She'd felt secure with him. Emotionally, physically. That, she thought, had been the beginning of the smooth-sailing part of her life, where she could relax and enjoy things. They'd even talked about buying a house together.

Then he'd lost his job.

She'd just settled into the new normalcy of that dynamic when she got hurt, upending her world.

Now…

She felt lost.

I hate this.

Underneath everything, the desperate hope that she didn't do something stupid and fall for John in some dumb-ass damsel in distress sort of way. The white knight swooping in and rescuing her from the brink.

Maintaining her emotional distance had to remain firmly in focus. Otherwise, she might make another stupid choice. Although Tom only looked like a stupid choice in retrospect. He'd accused her of changing, but maybe she hadn't. Maybe he had.

Or maybe he'd never been who she thought he was in the first place.

Too tired and hurt and in pain to think about it anymore, she took a long, hot shower before sliding under the covers.

Chapter Eight

John wondered why the hell his alarm was going off so early on a Sunday morning. He'd swatted at it, trying to silence it, when one thought broke through and pierced the bubble of sleep trying to hold on to him.

Abbey.

Tossing the covers back, he sat up, feet on the floor, and finally got the alarm silenced.

Abbey.

That got him moving. He'd promised to bring her breakfast, and he wanted to be there before the others arrived, so he could take charge and make sure she didn't overdo things. He'd seen the pinched, agonized look in her face, the way she tried to breathe through her pain when standing up or getting out of the car.

The way she leaned on the cane when on her feet.

That was a woman in a lot of agony and trying to hide it.

You're running from your own issues.

As he jumped in the shower he admitted that. Sure. A chance to help, to focus on something other than his own grief, a chance to *fix* something, to make a positive difference?

Hell, yes, this was a trade-off he'd welcome.

Gladly.

After getting his shower and dressing he headed out, stopping by a Dunkin' Donuts on the way for two boxes of coffee, a couple of bagel sandwiches to make sure Abbey would have a marginally decent breakfast, and a couple dozen assorted donuts for the crew. He pulled into her driveway five minutes before seven, surprised to realize how forward he was looking to this.

Not just the chance to help her out, but the chance to make something easier on her. To fix this for her in the only way he could.

Smiling, and feeling the first genuine bit of contentment since learning of Mick's death, he grabbed everything and headed up the walk to her front door.

* * * *

Used to getting up early for work, Abbey was awake even before her alarm went off at six. She winced as she stretched her arm to silence the damn thing.

When her mind briefly wondered where Tom the late weekend sleeper was, she remembered.

He hadn't even called or texted her yesterday to check on her, see how she was.

Yeah, he really *cares about me, all right.*

She bitterly wondered how long he'd spent online chatting last night with his new FetLife friend. When the thought of logging in to see what he was up to and track his movements came to mind, she shoved it away.

No. I will not *be crazy stalker lady. If he can walk away from me, I can walk away from him.*

As it always did now, it took her a couple of tries to log-roll herself into a position where she could push up with her arms so she was sitting on the side of the bed. And as it always did now, it was accompanied by lots of deep breathing in an attempt to control the pain.

Her thoughts once again went to the prescriptions in her purse. Maybe she needed to fill them.

I don't want *to.*

It was the last area of her life she had control over, how she dealt with her pain. Giving in and hoping medicine took care of it would be the final blow to her ego and dignity.

She started a pot of coffee and then went straight to the shower to soak under the hot spray. She didn't even care if she got her hair wet. It was only down to her shoulders, and lately she'd taken to wearing it either loose or pulled into a ponytail. Trying to take the effort to actually style it meant energy not there to deal with her pain. She was also overdue for a trip to the salon, and grey roots were showing here and there in her reddish auburn hair.

Sitting for a couple of hours in a chair in a salon wasn't exactly something she could do now. Not without a lot of pain involved.

I took my life for granted.

Her health, her job, her relationship—everything. She'd hit a comfortable point and assumed she'd always be there.

When she finished with her shower, she donned an oversized T-shirt and comfy, baggy shorts. No bra, the effort to put on one would hurt too much, and it wasn't like her friends weren't used to glimpsing boobies anyway. None of them would be shocked by her letting the girls hang free under her shirt.

At five till seven she heard a car out front and, remembering to grab the cane, made her way to the front door just in time to see John stepping onto the porch. He looked a little startled when she opened the door before he even had time to juggle everything around and knock or ring the bell.

She stepped aside. "Holy cow, what'd you bring?"

"Everything." He headed straight for the kitchen, setting the items on the counter. She shut the door and followed him.

"And I expect you to eat," he said, handing her a bag. "Ham, egg, and cheese on a plain bagel. Hope that's okay."

"That's…" She needed to clamp down on her emotions now or she'd be a blubbering mess all day.

Instead, she hugged him. "Thank you. I appreciate it."

"No worries." He looked pleased, happy. "Sit and eat, please."

Then again, he hadn't had the best couple of days himself. Maybe this was his way of compensating and taking his mind off his friend's death.

He'd purchased a sandwich for himself, too. After pouring her coffee and fixing it per her instructions, he settled on a barstool at the counter while she opted to stand.

"Isn't that hurting your back?"

"It's almost worse to get down and get up again. I promise," she added, forestalling the protests she anticipated, "that I will take it easy today." She stared out the sliders. "I'll work on trying to get George corralled and figure out how to best go about moving his stuff. Did you say the Collins brothers are helping?"

"Yes, Landry did. They've got a couple of pickup trucks. If you can tell me what needs to get moved into his kiddie pool, I'm sure that we can load everything into the back of a truck and put a tarp over it to keep it from getting blown out. We'll save moving him and his stuff toward the end, so you can get him transferred with the least amount of trauma to him. Do you have something to transport him in?"

"I have a pet carrier for him."

By the time they'd finished their breakfast sandwiches, Tilly, Landry, and Cris had arrived and the fun started. They unloaded the boxes and moving supplies out of Abbey's car. Cris, Landry, and John started packing things in the living room while Tilly helped her in the bedroom.

It took a little convincing on Abbey's part for Tilly not to dump Tom's clothes into the backyard and burn them, but she finally got her friend to leave all his stuff neatly stowed in the guest room dressers or closet or on the bed.

Abbey wouldn't fight dickishness with dickishness.

No matter how tempting it was.

Within an hour, they had ten more helpers, complete with trucks, and John was leading a caravan back to his house to start the unloading, as well as getting help moving the boxes out of the guest room into the garage so Abbey's furniture could be moved into it.

Cris set Abbey up in a chair in the kitchen to help people go through the cabinets there, one by one, and point out what went and what stayed behind. At lunchtime, someone brought in several pizzas and everyone took a break.

Abbey was shocked to realize they were almost completely done with moving everything out of her house, although the second half of the day, arranging her furniture in her new room, was waiting on her presence at John's.

Not her house, she reminded herself.

And this was Tom's house.

Despite what she'd thought over the past several years, what she'd believed to be true, it had never really been her house. Nor her home.

Maybe he really had loved her at some point, or believed he had. She'd loved him. She never would have moved in with him if she hadn't, giving up her privacy and independence to share a household with someone.

As she looked out into the living room, where John stood with a paper plate and a piece of pizza while smiling and talking with Tilly, Abbey realized, in a way, she was doing that again. Only without the illusion of love or a relationship. This would strictly be a roommates arrangement.

She wouldn't let it become more than that. She needed to get through her surgery and recovery and then find another place so she could put her life back together. Until then, both she and George would be living out of boxes in someone else's home.

It wouldn't be her home.

I haven't even told my family yet.

Ugh.

She could already hear her mother's voice in her head.

At least you weren't married to the son of a bitch. Did you get yourself tested for STDs yet? He was probably cheating on you.

Crap. That was something else she'd need to get done on top of everything else. No, she didn't believe Tom had physically cheated on her. Didn't want to believe it, anyway.

Then again, she'd also believed he was in love with her, loved her, so why should she take his word on that when so many other things had been a lie?

Essie, the fourth member of the Collins' brothers poly quad, joined her in the kitchen. "How you holding up?"

Why lie? "I'm so tired. I can't begin to tell everyone how much this means to me."

"Hey, you're family. I love your tortoise. Russian?"

"Yeah. That's right, you're a vet tech, aren't you?"

Essie smiled. "Was. Now they have me helping them out with the clients. They're even putting me on the TV show despite me trying to talk them out of it. I guess the network liked the ratings boost." The brothers owned a disaster recovery and commercial cleaning service, but they also did hoarding clean-outs, sometimes filmed by a cable network crew for a show they were part of.

"Do you miss it? Working with animals?"

"A little. I volunteer at the shelter a few times a month and help them out there. The trade-off has been worth it. So, Russian?"

Abbey realized her brain wasn't in gear with everything else going on. "Sorry, yes. Got him when he was a hatchling from a reputable breeder."

"Love his enclosure. Mind if I take pictures of it?"

"Go ahead. I hate having to disassemble it. He's really enjoyed it."

Abbey finished her pizza, grabbed some romaine from the fridge, and led Essie out onto the lanai. "Watch this." She dragged a chair over to the end and sat. "Hey, Georgie boy."

The tortoise lifted his head, slowly turned himself around, and headed toward her.

Essie let out a laugh. "Oh my god, that's adorable."

"He's twenty-one. People don't understand after a while, they get to know their owners and respond to them. They're not like a dog or a cat or a parrot even, but they have personalities."

Essie knelt next to the enclosure and watched as George stretched his neck to take a piece of romaine from Abbey.

"That's the most adorable thing I think I've seen." Essie pulled out her phone and took pictures of him, then of the enclosure. "Luckily, we've only had cat and dog hoarders. No reptiles so far. Does he get lonely?"

"They're solitary by nature. Some people have more than one, but I never had the room to have more than one." He took another piece of romaine from her. "Kind of like I should have stayed, I guess," Abbey mused. "Solitary."

When she saw the look of sympathy on Essie's face, she realized she'd said it out loud.

"Sorry," Abbey said. "Just throwing myself a pity party. Don't mind me."

"Don't worry about it. You've been through a lot." Her expression darkened. "Tilly won't be the only one wanting a crack at that asshole if he ever sets foot in the club again, believe me."

"I don't want him hurt. I just want this over so I can move on. Honestly."

Essie stood. "Hey, we're all here for you. When you have your surgery, it won't just be Tilly volunteering to help you out until you're back on your feet. If it's any consolation, one of the guys in our crew had to have back surgery, and he said he wished he'd had it done immediately instead of avoiding it and trying physical therapy first. Once the surgical pain started healing, he said he felt better than he had in the months leading up to the surgery."

"That's what everyone keeps telling me."

John joined them on the lanai. "We're ready to get started again, if you are."

Abbey dropped the rest of the lettuce into the water dish for George. It'd keep it from wilting as fast and encourage him to take a dip and soak for a few minutes. John and Essie helped her up and Abbey had to bite down on her lower lip to stifle the moan of pain.

He frowned. "Didn't they give you any painkillers?"

"Yeah, I have a prescription for them in my purse, but I don't want to take them."

"Why not?"

"I hate them."

He arched an eyebrow at her and then called out, "Tilly!"

She appeared in the open slider doorway. "Yo."

John handed Abbey off to Tilly. "Take Little Miss Stubborn here to the drugstore to get her pain meds filled. She has a prescription she hadn't gotten filled yet."

"What?"

Aw, shit. "That's not fair," Abbey complained.

John arched an eyebrow at her. "Who ever said I'd play fair?"

* * * *

John felt a little bad about ratting Abbey out to Tilly. But earlier that morning, as they were working together to clear Abbey's things out of the master bathroom, John had promised to tell Tilly if Abbey was holding anything back about her health.

This, as far as he was concerned, was holding back. Abbey's face looked drawn and haggard, dark circles under her eyes as she made tiny, shuffling movements, which only seemed to get worse as the day went on.

Tilly shuttled Abbey off the lanai, demanding to know where her friend's purse was and ordering her to head toward the front door.

Essie chuckled. "Aw, hell. Abbey's in trouble."

"She's going to be in more trouble if she doesn't listen to Tilly and follow her orders. That's a nurse with a mission, right there."

Meanwhile, John took a group over to his house to start organizing things there. They'd filled his garage after putting her bedroom set in the guest room, but hadn't gotten any farther than that. They'd been able to transport the dresser drawers separately without unpacking her clothes, so that was a timesaver. But he got help rearranging the guest room to make space for her bookshelves, and they unpacked several boxes.

Every bit that they could do that she didn't have to do would be less stress on her.

He realized, however, that with her bedroom set in the room, there wouldn't be room for George. So he enlisted more help rearranging his living room so the tortoise's indoor pool would fit in the corner close to the sofa, where Abbey could easily get to it.

By the time they returned to Abbey's, she looked a little ticked off at Tilly, who'd seated her on the sofa there with a bottle of water.

"It should hopefully start kicking in soon," Tilly told John.

"If it makes me puke," Abbey warned her, "you're cleaning it up."

"This is different stuff than you said you reacted to. At least give it a chance. If it takes care of some of the pain, and doesn't make you sick, then hey, at least it's helping."

"Tilly," he asked, "do I have your permission to go Dom on her ass if she doesn't listen to me about taking her meds?"

"Absofarkinglutely."

"Hey! Don't I get a say here?"

In unison, Tilly and John said, "No."

Tilly stuck out her hand to John for a fist bump, which he returned.

"Just be glad," Tilly said, "that we're getting along now." She wagged a finger at Abbey. "When you're all healed up, I'll let you get your revenge then, on both of us."

"Hey," John said.

Tilly grinned. "You think I'm letting her beat only my ass, think again, buddy. There is no I in team."

"But there is in pain," Abbey said, shooting them both a dark look.

John didn't care. At least she seemed to be thinking about something other than what that weaselly shit Tom had done to her.

And he and Tilly were now on the same team.

Team Abbey.

I'll take the win.

Chapter Nine

The painkillers didn't make Abbey sick, but they muddied her thoughts, making everything fuzzy in a way she didn't like. At least they took the edge off the pain.

After one final walk through the house to make sure everything was gone that belonged to her, it was time to tackle moving George. Tilly made Abbey sit in a chair on the lanai and direct everyone else's efforts. Essie gently captured George and put him in the pet carrier, on a towel, and handed it to Abbey to hold while everyone else started transferring dirt and substrate into the kiddie pool, along with the plants.

The Collins brothers also had several large plastic totes into which they were able to transfer the rest of the dirt, substrate, plants, and even sod from the enclosure, then the men worked on disassembling the sides. There wasn't anything they could do about the weed barrier cloth except rip it loose from the staples. Then, using a couple of the pieces of lumber to support the bottom of the kiddie pool, they moved everything out to a couple of pickup trucks.

John grabbed the hose and rinsed off the lanai while Tilly helped Abbey outside. She'd chauffeur Abbey and George back to John's place. Once everyone was out of the house, Abbey locked it.

"You going to leave the key here?" John asked.

"No, I'll need to come get the mail next week while he's gone," she said. "And I need to get my address changed anyway, so I'll still have to come by to get my mail." She stared at the house, trying to remember how it'd felt when she'd moved in.

She couldn't remember now.

Or, maybe it was the painkillers.

Back at John's house, she was nearly driven to tears of gratitude to see how John had rearranged the living room to accommodate George's pool. She got him settled in there, with John's help setting up George's lights. They stacked the lumber for his tortoise enclosure on John's lanai, along with the tubs of plants and dirt. John said he'd take care of them over the next couple of days.

Then the rest of the helpers who were still there started unpacking Abbey's belongings for her, the things they'd needed to wait for her input before they could take care of it. Stuff that she'd need now, versus items that could remain in boxes in the garage to await her next move. And Tony took care of setting up her TV and cable box for her in the bedroom so she didn't have to worry about it.

Tilly and Clarisse took over unpacking her bathroom supplies, while the men worked to finish arranging the bedroom the way she wanted it. By the time Abbey called it quits at seven and ordered more pizzas for everyone who was still there, there really wasn't much left for her to do. She had some dirty laundry she'd have to wash, but her friends had done all the hard work for her.

Another round of painkillers later, and she was sitting on John's sofa, Tilly on one side of her and John on the other, quietly studying her friends as they ate and talked.

Tilly gently nudged her. "Are you all right?"

"Yeah. I will be. Just…adjusting. I owe you all so much. Thank you for all of this. It's overwhelming and appreciated more than I can tell you."

"Hey," Cris said. "That's what family's for."

"God, I haven't even told my own family about my move yet. Crap. I'm not looking forward to that."

"Just tell them the truth," Tilly said.

"Oh, sure. 'Hey, my boyfriend's been chatting up a Domme in Dallas, and decided to leave me for a job out there.' They don't know anything about my kinky life and I'd rather keep it that way. They can remain blissfully unaware in their little bubbles of denial."

Tilly rolled her eyes. "*No*, you tell them he found a new job out there, but with everything going on, you can't move out there with him, so you decided to amicably part ways."

"Oh." That was so stupidly simple, Abbey didn't know why she hadn't seen it. "Sorry."

"Stop apologizing," Landry said. "This has been a rough few days on you. At least now with the move out of the way, you can focus on your health and getting better. When do you find out about the surgery?"

"I need to call the doctor's office tomorrow. I didn't hear back from them yet."

"Let me know as soon as you do," Tilly said. "You won't be alone." She covered Abbey's hand with hers. "I'm going to be there. I'm sure John will, too."

"Absolutely," John said.

Abbey turned to look at him. What did it say that a man she barely knew, whom she'd now be living with, had so quickly come to be someone she could depend on more than a man she'd actually lived with and had a relationship with for over four years, give or take?

And she did trust John. Askel and others had vouched for him. He had a good job, obviously was a great housekeeper, and had come through for her in a way for which she'd never be able to repay him.

And all that at a time in his own life when she wouldn't have blamed him if he'd wanted to retreat from the world for a while and spend his spare time grieving his friend.

"You're doing so much for me already," she said. "You don't need to take time off work for me."

He shrugged. "I have a shit-ton of vacation time stored up. Not like I was going anywhere. I'd be happy to take at least a couple of days off to get you through this."

She didn't know if it was the painkillers, or her overwhelmed emotions, or just her exhaustion, but she leaned over, tipping her head onto John's shoulder. "Thank you."

The others helped clean up the last of the pizza boxes and finished tidying up while Abbey sat there staring at George's temporary home and feeling useless. Poor George was doing counterclockwise laps in the plastic kiddie pool, following the edge of it around and around, going nowhere.

I know how you feel, dude.

* * * *

John was worried about Abbey, about her state of mind, but knew that unless she wanted to open up to him there wasn't much he could do except be there for her and support her as a friend.

Once everyone else left, he closed and locked the door and walked over to George's pool. The poor tortoise had already made a grooved path around the edges of the substrate in his makeshift home as he circled it.

"Is there anything I can do for him to help him settle down?" John asked.

"Just turn off his lights. He'll bed down eventually in his house, once he realizes it's night." John was doing that when he heard her grunt of pain and turned in time to see her using her cane to get up off the couch before he could make it over to help her.

"You could have asked for help."

"You've already done more than any person could reasonably expect."

"Are you going to work tomorrow?"

"I have to. I have meetings in the morning. I'll be done by two." She hobbled her way over to George's enclosure. "Sorry, buddy," she said, looking down at him. "Back to the small digs for a while."

"Can I get you anything? Or help you with anything?"

Her smile looked pained, weary. "No, thank you. I'll be okay. Sorry we're upending your life like this."

"You're not upending my life. It'll be nice having someone around to talk to for a change."

"I'll get cash out tomorrow for you for rent."

"You can give me a check. I trust you. And whenever."

"I'd rather do it sooner rather than later." She looked around, found her purse, and rummaged around in it for her checkbook.

"Abbey, this can wait until tomorrow. You look like you need to go rest. And you are welcomed to use the pool and hot tub whenever you want. I bet the hot tub would be good for your pain."

She hesitated, like she was trying to process what he'd just said.

Wow, she's really hurting. And probably a little bit of the painkillers messing with her, too.

"Okay." She shoved her checkbook back into her purse. "Maybe I should go to bed. I'm exhausted."

"Good night. Hope you get a good night's sleep."

"Thanks."

He waited until he heard her bedroom door close before he got started on his own preparations. The coffeepot, which he set to go off at six in the morning, ready when he got up. Then he made his lunch and put it in the fridge, ready to grab and go. He cleaned up the few dishes in the sink, put them into the dishwasher, and started it.

Down the hall, he heard the sound of Abbey's shower running.

Good. Maybe after a hot shower and a good night's sleep she'd feel a little better.

Looking around, he noted the differences with her presence. Her large furniture, like the dinette set, was stored out in the garage, along with boxes of kitchenware she wouldn't need here. But he'd made room for her recliner, and a small, decorative table, in the living room.

Actually, reconfigured the way it was, it looked better, less empty than it had before.

Her desk, along with bookshelves and other things, now shared room in his home office, which had been rearranged to accommodate her stuff. Slightly tight squeeze, but it worked.

As he walked down the hallway, he paused at her closed bedroom door. Besides the obvious, he sensed a seismic shift in his life. Had sensed it yesterday when talking with her at the club.

He usually wasn't a man to believe in any kind of woo-woo New Age stuff, wasn't religious by any stretch of the imagination.

But, somehow, there was something different. Like he'd stepped onto an unseen path and was now following it to a better place than he'd been headed before.

If nothing else, this weekend had been a blessed respite from having to think about Mick and the gaping void in his life as a result of his friend's death.

I hope this wasn't a mistake.

He headed to his own bedroom, closing the door behind him.

* * * *

Abbey stood under the spray as hot as she could tolerate it, her hands braced against the tile wall while the water hit her directly on her back. She knew it wouldn't make a lot of difference, but it would ease her pain enough to help her get to sleep.

Hopefully.

She didn't dare risk taking another one of the strong painkillers that night for fear of oversleeping in the morning. Plus she didn't want to drive while taking them. Not until she was more used to them. Her head felt stuffed full of cotton, her reflexes dulled.

She'd have to reserve those for the worst days.

Then again, today could classify as a worst day. On a scale of one to ten, her pain had been around a ninety. The worse pain yet, and no doubt exacerbated by the stress of the move as much as the actual physical activity related to it.

So much to do. There was an entire checklist of things she'd have to go through, change of address forms to get filled out, all of that.

Crap.

She might as well get a PO Box, since she'd be moving again in a few months. It'd be stupid to change it all just to have to change it again.

Her thoughts went back to John. She felt torn between irritation at him for teaming up with Tilly to get her prescription filled, and warm inside that he'd cared enough to pay attention to her pain.

Why the hell was I with Tom again?

Yeah, he'd ask her how she was, how she felt, but it always seemed more like he did it because he knew it was expected of him, not because he really worried about her.

Or am I being less charitable to him now that I'm moved out and really pissed off at him?

That could be, too. She wasn't an idiot.

A woman scorned, and all that.

The irony didn't escape her that Gilo and Tom had switched places on Tilly's shit list.

Well, the idiot's moving to Texas. Not like I'll ever have to see him again.

Finally, she climbed out of the shower, toweled off, and crawled into bed, naked. It took her a few minutes to get all her pillows arranged. With her back pain, she had to sleep on her right side with a pillow between her knees, another supporting her left thigh to keep her body from twisting, and one against her back to help brace her.

Finally arranged, she glanced over and realized she'd already set her alarm clock when she'd plugged it back in.

It's going to be weird going to sleep in a strange place.

But before she knew it, sleep had taken her.

Chapter Ten

When Abbey awoke Monday morning, her first thought was what the hell had happened. Besides her body being wracked with pain, she panicked for a moment that the dim, early morning light seeping through the blinds in her window was coming from the wrong direction. That maybe she'd slept all day and it was six at night and not morning.

As sleep finally fled her system, she remembered the move. This was her new home. Temporarily, at least.

I hate Tom.

Not in a want-to-castrate-him kind of way, with a Tilly level of psychopathy, but that he'd upended her life over his selfish desires.

Then again, if he was that selfish, she was better off without him.

Looking back on their conversation, Tom had said his original plan was to wait until after she was back on her feet. Maybe her life had been a lie for longer than she'd realized.

Maybe he'd been planning to leave for a while.

Maybe he hadn't been looking for a job quite as hard as he'd said he'd been.

Not that it matters now.

Those were not constructive thoughts, and right now the last thing she needed was to beat herself up mentally when her body already hurt worse than holy fuck in very bad ways.

Carefully, she went through her morning agony of untangling herself from her pillows and log-rolling herself into a sitting position. Once she got that far, she knew she could get herself up and moving again.

This surgery can't happen soon enough for me.

She'd never had major surgery. Hell, never even needed stitches before. The thought of them cutting into her spine terrified the everliving fuck out of her. The thought of being knocked out and helpless.

The thought of not being able to care for herself in the early days of her recovery.

Well, I can barely care for myself now.

She was glad to smell coffee brewing and realized that she had no idea where John kept his mugs, or the sugar and creamer, in his kitchen. Or if he even had any.

I need to go back to the house today after work and clean out the fridge and pantry. Not everything, but her stuff. While she'd wanted to make sure she'd moved all her pots and pans and utensils, she hadn't thought about the food.

With Tom gone for a week, some stuff in the fridge would go bad anyway.

Might as well bring it here and use it up.

She pulled on a robe over her naked body and slowly made her way to her bedroom door. As she walked down the hall, she noticed the mixed glow of UVB and basking lights illuminating the corner of the living room. When she reached the kitchen, she spotted John standing there, reading the newspaper and wearing a robe. His brown hair was tousled and he looked half-asleep.

"Good morning," she said, grateful to know she wouldn't have to hunt all over to make her coffee. "You get a real paper?"

He smiled. "I know. One of my little pleasures I refuse to give up." He turned and pulled a coffee mug down from a cabinet and retrieved a spoon from a drawer for her. "I didn't think to ask if you have a favorite mug or something that got packed. I'll dig it out for you, if you'd like."

"No, not really." He'd put out creamer, sugar, and artificial sweeteners on the counter for her.

"There's milk in the fridge, too."

"Thanks." She was aware of him watching how she made her coffee. "What?"

He smiled. "Nothing. Thanks for trusting me and letting me help you."

"I'm the one thanking you."

He shrugged. "I like being helpful." A dark, foggy expression crossed his face. "I haven't felt very helpful the past few days. I've felt helpless. At least this was something I could do. A way to make things right."

She sipped at her coffee, glad to discover he made it strong, the way she liked it, and not watered down the way Tom always had despite her repeated attempts to tell him to use more grounds.

"I'm really sorry about your friend."

"Thanks. It's life, though. The older we get, the more friends we lose like that." He nodded to her mug. "Is it okay? If you like it weaker or stronger, let me know."

"It's perfect, thank you." Her eyes met his for a moment. She felt like maybe something passed between them, but she couldn't put her finger on it. "Do you get up this early every morning?"

"Yep. Usually, I put the TV on and listen to the news while I get ready, but I didn't want to wake you up."

"That's okay. I like to listen to the news, too. Please don't change how you live just because I'm here."

A playful smile lit his face. "Then I'll have to warn you I enjoy skinny-dipping in the pool and hot tub."

It felt good to laugh. "That neither surprises nor shocks me. Knock yourself out. Who knows? I might join you some nights."

"Your company is always welcomed."

"Thanks." She walked over to George's pool and realized the tortoise was still dug in for the night. Carefully, she reached in and got his water dish out, took it into the hall bathroom, and rinsed and refilled it before replacing it in the enclosure. He had plenty of grazing plants, so she didn't need to supplement his food that morning. She'd give him his romaine that afternoon. After checking everything, she returned to the kitchen and washed her hands with soap and water.

"Can I ask a stupid question?" John started.

"Sure."

"Why didn't you just do that in the sink here?"

"While I've never had a problem, there is a slight risk of salmonella with them. I don't like to clean his stuff in the kitchen sink. So if you ever see lettuce floating in the toilet bowl, it's probably because I dumped his old food out before I washed the bowl in the bathroom sink."

John chuckled. "Thanks for the warning."

He glanced at the time and picked up his coffee mug. "Well, I have to get ready. If you need anything and can't find it, feel free to come into my room and holler at me through the bathroom door. And don't worry about showering at the same time I do. I have a large hot water tank, and the master bath has a self-contained on-demand water heater anyway."

That was going to be her next question. "I get the feeling we're going to settle into a comfortable routine fairly fast."

"I hope so. It's nice having someone around." He patted her on the shoulder as he eased past her and headed back down the hall.

The way he'd said it…

No. Don't read anything into it. He's a nice guy, yes, but you just went through a breakup. Don't be an idiot. Don't go throwing yourself at him.

She sipped her coffee, waiting until she heard his bedroom door shut before painfully shuffling back down the hall to her room.

It wasn't until she'd closed the bedroom door that she finally processed the fact John had already turned on the lights over George's enclosure before she ever made it out to the kitchen in the first place.

* * * *

John hoped his morning woody hadn't been poking at the front of his robe too much. He'd heard Abbey's door open and barely got himself turned around and facing the counter before she'd walked into the kitchen.

Of course little probably shocks her.

True, but he didn't want to come off as a raging dick with his raging dick making her rethink her decision to move in with him.

He wasn't lying. It was nice to have someone else around, even if just as a roommate. Yes, he had some acquaintances, mostly from work, whom he hung out with sometimes. A couple of neighbors were very nice. Scattered friends here and there.

But none of them had known the real him, the hidden part he kept isolated.

For the first time, he had someone in his life who not only knew about that part, but didn't mind. Hell, didn't *care*.

Someone with whom he didn't have to hide his true self. Someone he didn't have to worry about finding his toy bag or his fetish clothes. Someone he didn't have to lie to and say the folded spanking bench buried behind wooden hurricane panels in his garage was actually a sawhorse.

Someone who wouldn't care if she opened his closet and spotted a tube full of canes, riding crops, and other implements.

It felt freeing, in a way.

After showering and dressing, he returned to the kitchen to eat a yogurt for breakfast and fill his travel mug with coffee. Abbey rejoined him a few minutes later, looking smart in a pair of slacks and a blouse with a blazer.

She cocked her head at him, a playful smile teasing her lips. "Did I ever tell you I have a suit fetish?"

Well, he wasn't wearing a suit. Today he wore khakis, loafers, a long-sleeved button up shirt, and a tie. Fairly standard. He did have a blazer he'd take with him in case he needed to do an on-camera interview or sit in a meeting with higher-ups, but usually he didn't need it.

"You do, huh?"

She nodded, that playful smile melting places inside him he hadn't realized had been frozen over. "You look good."

"I clean up well."

"What story are we going to agree to tell the 'nillas about us?" she asked. "About how we ended up living together."

He shrugged. "I always go for the simplest option. You were a friend thrust into a situation through no fault of your own, I had the space, and you needed a roommate."

"Works for me." She headed for the coffeemaker.

"What would you like for dinner tonight, by the way?"

She turned. "You don't have to cook for me."

"I know I don't have to, but I want to. I have to make myself dinner anyway. It's silly to cook only for one."

"I'm not picky. I'm not fond of curry, but I'll eat pretty much anything else. No food allergies."

"Good. None for me, either. Any other allergies I need to know about?"

"Yeah. I'm allergic to bullshitting ex-boyfriends who claim they love me but are willing to leave without even bothering to see if I'm okay." She burst into tears.

He froze, processing for a second before stepping over to her and pulling her into his arms.

"Shh, it's okay. Just let it out."

"I'm sorry. I didn't want to do this, to break down like this. You've been so nice to me and here I am blubbering all over you."

He stroked her hair, which she'd worn loose. She smelled good, flowery something, probably her shampoo, if he had to guess. He closed his eyes and took a deep breath while praying his erection didn't decide to make a grand entrance.

"Hey, like I said, I'm a fixer. I live to make things right for people. You're helping me out by being here. I feel useful. Let me be useful, please?"

She relaxed against him, her arms encircling him. A sense of peace settled over him as they stood there. In his mind an image slammed into sharp focus, of him on his knees at her side, her fingers twined in his hair, his cheek resting against her thigh, awaiting her command.

Her voice floated through her mind, of what she'd said. *I have a suit fetish.*

Aaannnd that was when his cock woke up again.

Shit.

Adjusting position would only make it more obvious, so he hoped she didn't realize what was going on.

After a few minutes, she finally released him and grabbed a piece of paper towel to blow her nose. That was when he realized she wasn't wearing any makeup.

Not that she needed any. She was beautiful without it.

"Better?" he asked.

She nodded, meeting his gaze. She had beautiful green eyes. "Thank you. I swear I'll get my emotions under control here in the next few days."

"Like I said, being helpful is my thing. Hell, it's *my* fetish." That drew a smile from her, warming his heart and twisting his soul. "I'll wear suits if you'll let me be helpful."

Aaannd a full-on smile from her.

Score.

"Deal," she said, leaning and kissing him on the cheek. "Thanks."

* * * *

Despite her pain, Abbey's missing libido had come screaming back to life when she felt the size of John's bulge pressing against her.

Holy crap!

She'd never seen John naked. The few times she'd scened with him, and any other time she'd seen him bottom to someone, he'd always worn a leather jock. He could have been hung like an elephant or a Chihuahua, for all she knew.

Apparently, he swung toward the tripod end of the scale.

Okay, don't think about that now, stupid.

It felt nice having him comfort her.

It'd felt even nicer knowing he was having that reaction to her, because, *hello*, he looked *damned* handsome in his work clothes.

But he didn't acknowledge it, and neither did she. She wasn't sure what the protocol was for asking your kinky roommate if they wanted to be play partners—or more—but she knew emotionally that was a conversation she needed to wait on until she wasn't feeling quite so…emotionally charbroiled.

Rebounding had never been her thing, and she wasn't about to start now. Whether poor judgment on her part for not seeing the signs with Tom, or just ignorance because he hid things well, she needed to sort all that out in her mind before she even thought about approaching John. At least they had prior play sessions, so it wouldn't be a totally out-of-the-blue and awkward discussion.

When she finally had it with him.

But not now. It was too soon.

She left the house before he did, earlier than she normally left but unsure of what her morning commute time would be now that she had to take a different route.

As she drove, she thought about what John would look like spread out and tied to a St. Andrew's cross as she slowly unbuttoned his shirt and slacks to play with him.

Heellooo.

At least, it would seem, her libido wasn't as dormant as she'd thought.

Even if there wasn't anything she could do about it, it was still among the land of the living and not dead on arrival.

Thank god for that.

Chapter Eleven

John's Monday was the usual crazy mix of weirdness from the weekend, stuff that warranted a report but not a call-out to him or any of the other department heads. Minor shit-happens accidents as well as stupid human mistakes.

He opted to sit in his office for lunch after filling his water bottle from the cooler down the hall. While he ate, he ran a Google search for Russian tortoises. By the end of his lunch break, he'd learned more than he'd ever thought he'd know about the critters, including their diets.

And he now realized how dedicated Abbey was to her pet. She had created an environment for George where he could graze in as natural a way as possible.

He also couldn't stop replaying the kiss on the cheek she'd given him.

Why am I torturing myself?

Ah, because I'm a masochist. Duh.

He was glad he'd read through the tortoise information, because he usually kept fresh spinach in the fridge for salads, but the information said no to that food. He would have fed it to the tortoise without knowing it was bad for him.

I'm going to have to talk with her and get a list. He wanted to make sure when shopping that he didn't get George the wrong things.

Dell stopped by his office just after lunch. "How'd the interview go?" John asked. He hadn't even thought to look for the interview online.

"Thanks for the prep work. It saved my ass." Dell looked vaguely uncomfortable for a moment. "I'm sorry again about your friend."

John shrugged. He'd actually done a pretty decent job of keeping his mind off Mick all morning. "Thanks. It happens to all of us eventually."

"If you need anything…"

That was one of the usual platitudes, wasn't it? *Call me if you need me. Let me know if I can help. Please don't hesitate…*

But people usually didn't call, and the platitudes were, mostly, issued with full cognizance of that fact, even if only at a subconscious level and with all good intentions at the forefront of people's minds.

"Thanks," John said. "I'll be okay." Now he couldn't wait for Dell to leave. All he wanted to do was get back to work, get his mind focused on his job again, and not on Mick.

Hell, if he could just keep it focused on Abbey, or even George, that would be better than thinking about Nancy and her kids' grief on Saturday. Grief he'd basically bolted from, escaping to Venture.

It's going to be a long Monday.

* * * *

It would be a long damn Monday for Abbey. Late Friday, someone had tacked on another meeting to Abbey's calendar and she hadn't checked her work phone over the weekend to see the alert. It wasn't something she could slough off, either. Someone who hadn't realized she was supposed to be on limited work hours had set it up. It would keep her there at the office until nearly four.

Dammit.

She thought about the bottle of painkillers in her purse and knew she had to settle for the over-the-counter stuff for now. By the time she left work, it'd be close to rush hour and the last thing she needed was trying to negotiate heavy traffic with that crap in her system.

A little after lunchtime, her personal cell vibrated with a text message.

From Tom.

I'm in Dallas. Flight went well. Everything okay?

In disbelief she stared at the message. *What the unholy* hell*? How the* hell *am I supposed to respond to* that*?*

Her thumb hovered over the message, not sure whether to reply or swipe and delete it. Just because he was an asshole didn't mean she couldn't be the better person.

I can't do this right now.

She started to put her phone away when it buzzed again.

This time, it was a text from John.

How are you doing? Are you okay? Using your cane?

She had to cover her mouth with her hand to hold back the soft sob.

Here was a guy she barely knew, but who seemed more concerned for her than a guy who'd claimed to love and care for her for years.

After a couple of deep breaths to get her emotions under control, she replied to John's text.

Some jerk put a meeting on my calendar late Friday after I left for today. I'm stuck here until 4.

He responded almost immediately.

Will you be okay to drive or do you want me to come pick you up?

If John didn't stop being such a nice guy, she was going to end up a slobbery puddle of tears right there in her office.

I'll be okay, tks.

Another reply.

Text me when you leave, and when you get home, if I'm not there already.

Under normal circumstances, it would have rankled her, her natural assumption that he was trying to keep tabs on her.

Except she knew why he was doing that.

He was genuinely concerned about her.

If he didn't settle down after a few days and relax, she'd have a gentle conversation with him about it. Right now, she suspected Tilly had given him orders to keep a close watch on her and report any problems immediately.

Considering how her friends had all put themselves out on her behalf that weekend, she wasn't about to respond with snark or bitchiness.

Thank you. I will. :)

And in all honesty, it felt good to have someone genuinely concerned about her for a change.

One more text from John.

:)

That made her smile.

She stared at Tom's text one last time, opting to respond.

I'm fine.

Then she returned her phone to her purse and got back to work. Tom didn't deserve any more response than that from her.

He dang sure didn't deserve her attention.

* * * *

John was still at his desk late Monday afternoon when his personal phone vibrated with an incoming text message from Abbey.

FINALLY on my way home.

He frowned. It was almost five. He wasn't sure exactly where her office was, but knew the general vicinity and suspected she'd end up hitting nasty traffic snarls on the way home. Depending on how his day went, he either got in early and left early enough to beat the worst of the traffic, or he worked late until it'd had a chance to settle down before heading home. Otherwise, he could easily count on an extra thirty or more minutes tacked onto his drive time. Those were minutes better spent clearing e-mails or reviewing reports.

Text me when you get home.

She replied a moment later.

Will do.

Darn it. He'd wanted to try to time his arrival so he could cook her dinner and not make her wait. But he still had a good twenty minutes at least before he could get out of there.

He was in traffic when she texted him that she was home, and was going to take a pain pill and lie down for a little while. Which he thought was a great idea.

By the time he got home it was after six thirty and he was careful not to make a lot of noise coming in the front door. But when he went to drop his laptop case on the couch, he almost let go of it before realizing Abbey was sound asleep on the couch, in a T-shirt and shorts, the evening news playing on the TV.

Aww.

He could have stood there for hours just watching her. She looked vulnerable, sleep at least removing some of the pained, pinched lines from her features.

Now trying to be even quieter, he took his laptop to the bedroom and dumped it on his bed before returning to the kitchen to wash his travel mug and lunch container. Normally, he'd strip naked before making himself dinner.

Not today.

Maybe once they'd lived together for a while and they'd talked about it first and he knew she was comfortable with that.

Today, he left his work clothes on, with the exception that he removed his shoes and socks, before starting dinner. He'd opted for easy, baked chicken breasts and roasted veggies, with a side salad. After getting the chicken in the oven, he walked over to George's enclosure to check on him.

The tortoise raised his head when he saw John and started toward him.

Something about romaine.

He went to the fridge and found one of the two clear plastic tubs she'd stored in the bottom. On it, written in black permanent marker, it said GEORGE FOOD - ROMAINE. DO NOT EAT. The other was marked similarly, except it said ASSORTED GREENS.

He pulled a couple of pieces of romaine out and walked over to where George was now futilely trying to climb up the slick, sloped side of the plastic kiddie pool.

"Here you go, buddy," he whispered to him as he handed him a small piece.

To his delight, the tortoise nosed at it, then opened his mouth and took it from him, dropping back down onto all fours while munching it.

He would have sat there feeding George all night if it hadn't been for the soft sound of Abbey's voice a few minutes later. "Hey, sorry. I didn't hear you come in."

He looked over his shoulder at her. The pain had returned to her eyes. "That's because I was trying not to wake you up."

"What smells so good?"

"Chicken."

She didn't sit up. He wondered if she even could. "Thank you for giving him that. I just…I'm a horrible mommy. I got home and took a pill and sat down for a minute to try to rest and…"

"It's okay. George and I have it covered."

"He can't have spinach."

"I know. I looked it up. I gave him romaine from the tub."

"You looked it up?"

"Guilty. I spent my lunch hour giving myself a crash course in Russian tortoises. But I still want you to go through stuff with me."

He couldn't interpret the expression on her face. "How long have you been home?" she asked.

"About a half hour."

"You're still in your work clothes."

He hoped his smirk looked playful and not lecherous. "Someone said something about a suit fetish. I don't have a problem being objectified."

And there came a soft, pained laugh. "How do you normally dress after you get home?"

"I don't. But I figured instead of shocking you by you waking up to a naked guy running around here, I'd go for titillation." He flapped his tie at her.

That coaxed a genuine laugh from her. When she winced as she tried to sit up, he hurried over to help her. "Hey, where do you think you're going?"

"I was going to help you with dinner."

"Uh-uh. You're sitting here on this couch and chilling out. I'll bring you your dinner when it's ready. I eat on the couch all the time."

"I hurt so bad and I'm so tired I won't even argue with you tonight."

"Good."

"Did Tilly tell you to take care of me?"

He smiled. "She didn't have to. Remember, I like to fix things and be helpful. That's *my* fetish."

* * * *

Tilly called Abbey a little after eight that evening. Abbey had just gotten herself into a comfortable position on the couch and didn't feel like moving to grab her phone from the coffee table. John, however, lunged for it and handed it to her without looking at the screen.

"Thank you," she said, mentally filing that away.

Tom had always looked at the screen before handing her phone over, something that had annoyed the crap out of her but she'd never brought up, thinking it was just her hang-up.

"Hey," Abbey answered.

"Do I need to come kill him yet?"

She managed a laugh as she looked across the table at John, where he was settling back into her recliner. "No, we're fine. He's been super sweet. Thank you for all the times you didn't kill him."

He grinned.

"Yeah," Tilly said, "well, most of those times you can thank Cris or Landry for holding me back." Her tone turned serious. "But…really? Everything's okay? I'm ten minutes away."

"I'm fine. I took a pain pill after I got home and he made me dinner."

"Aww. I mean, oh, okay. Good."

Abbey did her best not to laugh at Tilly. She knew her friend put on a really good act in public for everyone, but had a soft heart well-protected inside that spiked exterior shell. "So promise me you won't hurt him unless I tell you to."

Here came the exaggerated sigh of aggravation. "Okay, *fine*. Be that way." Abbey could hear the smile on her friend's face.

"You can hurt Tom if he shows back up. How's that sound?"

"Like a damn fine plan. I'll even let John help hold him down."

"I'm sure he'd enjoy that." She glanced over at him, smiling at his furrowed brow.

"Okay. I'll check on you tomorrow. If you need me to go with you to your doctor appointments, let me know. I'll clear my schedule for you."

"Thanks, Til. Love ya."

"Love ya, too, sweetie."

Abbey ended the call. "Tilly said she'd let you help hold Tom down."

"Ah. You're right. I would enjoy that."

"See? I figured as much."

"Did you find out about your surgery yet?"

"Aw, dammit." She punched a reminder into her phone. "I was so busy I forgot to call them."

"You realize how much trouble you're in right now, right?" He wore a playful smile.

"What'd I do?" she asked.

"You've got not just Tilly riding your ass, but me, too."

I wouldn't mind him riding my ass.

She shoved that thought out of the way. Yes, he was a handsome man. No, right now was not the time to think lecherous thoughts about him.

"I'm not complaining," she said.

"Yet." He grinned.

She had just enough energy in her to toss a playful comment at him. "Are you trying to earn cane strokes for after I'm better?"

His smile widened. "Oooh. Want me to start a chart?"

It felt comfortable bantering with him. Playful.

Right.

Like she knew she could banter with him without it suddenly turning into him pressing her for more, and then getting petulant when it didn't.

Like…

Shit.

Like with Tom.

There would be some deep soul-searching in her immediate future. She needed to take a long, hard, honest look at her dynamic and relationship with Tom. To see what problems lay there, what she'd overlooked at the time and what—if anything—she was exaggerating now because of her raw and angry heart.

Already she knew the picture wasn't pretty. She'd let Tom walk all over her in many ways. Early on, Tilly had made a couple of roundabout comments on the subject, then dropped it. Abbey had assumed if it really was a problem, Tilly would have hounded her.

Tilly was many things. Shy about voicing her opinion when she worried about her friends was not one of them.

"Sure," Abbey said. "If you feel like it. Be careful what you wish for."

He laughed and settled back in the recliner. Yes, easy and peaceful.

Not hovering in the bad way, as if expecting her to follow through on the banter right that second.

After sending herself the reminder to check in with the doctor, she settled back to finish watching the TV show they'd turned on.

Chapter Twelve

Tuesday morning, Abbey placed her call to the doctor's office and found out her surgery was scheduled for two weeks from tomorrow. They'd had a cancellation and were able to fit her in sooner than they'd originally thought. It'd be on a Wednesday.

Greeaaat.

After ending the call, she looked at the sticky note where she'd jotted the information. She'd have a pre-surgical consult appointment a week from Wednesday to have bloodwork done and for them to go over the pre-op procedure with her. She'd have a special soap she'd have to scrub with, and of course she wouldn't be able to eat or drink after midnight the night before.

It also meant she wouldn't be able to clear all her current projects before taking time off for the surgery.

Dammit.

With the note in hand, she headed to her supervisor's office to go over everything with him and make the arrangements. She'd have to scramble and put in more hours than she was technically supposed to if she didn't want to leave a mess behind for someone to try to figure out while she was gone.

At least I'll still have a job when I come back in a few weeks.

That was something. She'd been with the company for over eleven years. Other than this whole incident, she had an unblemished record, rarely took a sick day, and had a personnel folder filled with glowing annual reviews and client reports.

By the time she slowly made her way downstairs early that afternoon, once the hectic day had been put behind her, she felt more sadness settle over her like an itchy, heavy, wet, smelly blanket. She liked to work, loved her job, enjoyed the majority of her coworkers.

Being forced to slow down not only pinched her pride, it made her realize she didn't have much of a life outside of work.

Other than her BDSM pursuits.

Well, and George, but he didn't count. He was her baby, not a hobby.

She got into the car and had already started driving toward Tom's house before she realized what she was doing.

Dammit.

Well, she did need to go there, to check the mail.

When she pulled into the driveway, she sat there for a moment and stared at the house. Already it felt…strange to her. Different.

Not as if she'd spent the past four years living there, and a frequent visitor even before that.

John had made her feel at home immediately.

What the hell have I been doing with my life?

Using her cane, she checked the mailbox and added a few more things to her mental list. In addition to forwarding her mail and getting a PO Box, she'd need to change the address on her auto insurance, her driver's license, and her car registration. Her voter ID.

Dammit.

More money, at least for the registration and license changes. Not to mention aggravation over wasted time at the DMV.

When she walked in, she realized she hadn't set the AC to a higher temp when she left on Sunday. Rectifying that, she grabbed a couple of plastic grocery bags and started emptying stuff from the fridge and freezer to take to John's.

While they were moving stuff on Sunday, someone had taken the time to clean up in their wake, vacuuming and sweeping and scrubbing so at least it didn't look like a hurricane had hit the place. One less thing she had to worry about.

The master bedroom looked empty, the bathroom spotless. All

that was left in the master bedroom was the unplugged cable box, sitting on the floor where the TV had been on the dresser, and a few of Tom's things still in the closet.

She left the closet door standing open so he wouldn't overlook the items still in there.

The house didn't have an attic. But even in the garage, as she'd pointed out what was hers and what wasn't, things had been shifted over to one side, Tom's things, leaving no trace behind of her presence.

Tilly and Clarisse had helped her go through Christmas and other holiday decorations, too. Everything.

Her friends were thorough. A job she'd dreaded had been accomplished in a few hours. Had Tom done it, it would have—

She cut off that line of thinking. Yes, she would have had to double- and triple-check Tom's work, knowing he would have screwed stuff up. Things overlooked.

She probably would have been getting calls right up until his own move date that he'd found something else of hers.

In this house, there was nothing remaining of her except her memories and her pain.

God, I'm depressing.

She still felt bad about George. The poor guy had been upended from his happy home and forced to downsize, too. Through no fault of his own.

Enough whining, girl.

She loaded the groceries into her car and this time got it pointed in the direction she intended to go, with a brief stop by the local PO first. She filled out a mail forwarding request to send everything to John's house for now, not wanting to wait in line to get a PO Box today.

All she wanted to do was take a pain pill and lie down.

George was doing laps in his enclosure when she returned home. "I know, buddy. I'm sorry." She put the groceries away, took a pain pill, then grabbed some romaine and sat in the chair next to his enclosure.

He cut across the middle of the kiddie pool and straight to her when he realized what she had in her hand.

"Just a few weeks, dude," she said, feeding him his daily treat. "Then we'll figure out what to do from there." The thought of finding an apartment was daunting enough. She knew most places would waive a pet fee for a tortoise. It wasn't like a cat or a dog. No noise, no destruction, no disturbance, no fur or dander.

But the thought of having to find a new apartment...

Maybe the pain pill had already started kicking in, but just thinking about the process made her want to cry. A house on her own was out of the question. She could probably swing the expense, but the maintenance was beyond her. She'd lived in her apartment before she'd met Tom for six years, with no problems. She wasn't a nomadic kind of person. Once she settled into a place, she didn't want to move. She needed to make sure she found a place she'd be happy in.

That was why her next move had to be carefully researched, studied, the costs tallied...

Sigh.

I wonder if they have any openings at the place I rented from before.

Okay, so yes, there was a good reason she was successful at her job. Her analytical mind made her a damn good operations research analyst.

So why the *hell* was she in the fix she found herself in?

After George finished his treat, she washed her hands, changed into comfy clothes, and let the pain pill's effects lull her into a nap on the sofa in front of the TV.

* * * *

John managed to get out of work early Tuesday, hoping to beat Abbey home and get a look at the pieces of George's large enclosure to see what he could figure out without her protesting that she didn't want him going through the trouble.

But when he made the final turn onto his street, he spotted her car in the drive.

Dang.

When he pulled in, he let the car run and turned off the radio. Then he used his work cell to call his supervisor and ask for the day off tomorrow. He used Abbey as an excuse, that she had a doctor's appointment.

It wasn't a problem, because he didn't have any meetings on the calendar and plenty of PTO time he hadn't even dipped into yet. He could cover his e-mail from home, and they could call him if they needed something.

He wanted to surprise her, to get George settled into a new lanai enclosure. John knew he might be jumping the gun, but he wanted to give Abbey every reason not to want to move again after she healed from her surgery. At least, not immediately.

That maybe, once she'd healed and could focus on something else, maybe she'd want to focus on him. On seeing if there was a chance for them to have a relationship.

He had kicked himself in the ass for the past four years, that he'd taken time away from Venture and ended up losing a chance to build something with Abbey. But at the time, work had been crazy, a series of public incidents, as well as hearings and protests on rate hikes, and he hadn't wanted to tempt fate and risk exposure.

By the time he'd made it back to the club, she was an item with Tom and his chance had passed.

This time, he wouldn't give up without a fight.

And if part of that fight was building the best damned tortoise enclosure in the state of Florida, he'd gladly roll up his sleeves and do it.

* * * *

Wednesday afternoon, Abbey sat in her car after leaving work and cried. With the AC blowing in her face, and her head resting on her hands on the steering wheel, she sobbed her heart out. Over her pain, over her situation...

Over the fact that a man who claimed to love her could so easily turn his back on her and walk away, while a man who was almost a stranger could open his home to her and suddenly become akin to family.

And she wasn't even sure what to do with *that*, with the conflicted emotions she was starting to have about John.

She wanted this out of her system now, before John got home later. Her emotions had hit critical mass in her brain when one of the administrative assistants, who hadn't heard about her sudden life change, asked how Tom was when Abbey was in HR and filling out change of address paperwork.

It'd taken every ounce of will she'd had not to burst into screaming tears right there.

Sitting there, it took Abbey a good fifteen minutes to get it out of her system. She knew if she went home and broke down crying and John was home that he would hear her and want to fix it for her.

And likely tell Tilly.

Which might mean interstate felony assault charges for Tilly if she hunted Tom down in Dallas and ripped his balls off over it.

Prison orange is not *Tilly's color.*

That was something Abbey had to keep reminding herself when she questioned *why*, exactly, she was holding her friend back from extracting revenge on Tom.

She stopped by Tom's house first—she couldn't think of it as her house anymore—and checked the mail. She took his inside and left it on the counter, where she'd left his other mail, and didn't linger.

There was no reason to.

When she returned to John's, she pulled into the driveway, into her now-usual spot, and shut the car off.

Home.

Maybe she'd even have a little energy to try to cook dinner for John. He'd texted her during the morning to check on her.

Nothing from Tom.

Then again, why would she expect anything from Tom? Why did she even *want* him to text her? So she could delight in not wanting to text him back?

Man, I have issues.

She went inside, took a pain pill, and changed clothes. Before she settled herself on the couch, she grabbed some romaine and headed for George's enclosure.

At first, she thought he was in his house. She called for him, but he didn't come out. When she gritted her teeth and leaned in to lift the house, he wasn't there.

"George?" She started digging through the substrate, raking it with her fingers, thinking maybe he'd dug himself in or something, but he wasn't there.

Now fear set in. "George?" She walked around the house, even opening John's bedroom door and going in there to see if she could find him.

No George.

With a lot of pain, she got down on her hands and knees and looked under the couch, under the chairs, under the table, under her own bed since her bedroom door had been open.

No George.

Panic, and now tears, set in.

She fumbled at the sliding glass doors and threw them open, terrified that somehow, he might have gotten out and into the pool, when—

She froze. Only because she realized the table and chairs that had been in the far corner of the lanai were now moved and wedged in between the hot tub and the pool.

At the far end of the lanai where the table and chairs used to be, apparently not complete but in progress, lay George's outside enclosure.

In progress, because it was twice as big and now an L-shape, and was only half-filled with substrate and plants from the plastic storage tubs. Positioned partly under the roof overhang, and partly in the sun, not only had John enlarged the enclosure, he'd put new weed barrier cloth underneath it, with hardware cloth under that for strength and support. She knew that because George was currently sunning himself on a patch of the black weed barrier and the hardware cloth was barely visible underneath it. It looked like John had wrapped it around the edges on the outside of the wood frame and stapled it into place.

That was where John found her standing ten minutes later when he arrived, unexpected and dressed in shorts and a T-shirt. He caught her just as she'd managed to stop crying, but the sight of him let loose another flood of tears.

He walked over, arms open. She let him pull her in for a hug, unable to express her gratitude.

He kissed the top of her head. "You're welcome," he said. "Dang, I thought I'd have more time before you got home to get it finished."

"I was looking all over the house for him because I thought he got loose and...thank you."

"Sorry. We were going to surprise you. I even got George a bow to put on his shell."

That started her laughing. "This is...I'll pay you back."

"No, you won't. I wanted to do this for him. I felt bad about him doing laps in that other one. I figured I'd be going a little stir-crazy, too, if I suddenly got downsized like that." He dragged a chair over for her from the table and went to get the romaine lettuce from where she'd dropped it on the counter when she realized George was MIA.

Then she watched as John hauled in several more bags of topsoil, coconut coir, and three more paving stones to make basking rocks for George.

"How did you know what to put in there?" she asked.

"I researched. Hey, Tortoise Town has to be right."

"Tortoise Town?"

"Yep. That's what I'm calling it."

"Did you take the day off work just to do this?"

"Yep." He smiled up at her from where he was transferring plants from the indoor enclosure. "I needed a day off anyway. I feel bad I gave you a scare."

"No, don't worry about it. This is just…I have no words."

So. Many. Ellipses.

Her thoughts had drifted past the point of knowing what to say to him. She was left with being forced to do little more than simply process.

She didn't have words. John had rendered her speechless.

Wait until I tell Tilly.

He'd even made provisions for the UVB and basking lamps and set them on a timer, hooked to an apparently new electrical outlet he'd installed along the back wall with external conduit.

"Been meaning to add another couple of outlets out here anyway," he joked.

"I have no idea how to thank you for this."

His smile widened. "You just did. Like I said, fixing things, making them better, that's *my* fetish. It was my pleasure to do this for you. And George. I'm already working on what we can do to improve the house for him when it gets colder this winter. I'm going to install a heat lamp, but set it on a temperature-sensitive switch so it'll automatically trip and turn on if it gets too cold."

"They make such a thing?"

"Sure."

She watched him work. Realization hit, and she spoke the words before she thought about them. The pain pill, probably. "This is how you're avoiding your grief, isn't it?" she quietly asked. "Over your friend."

His shoulders tensed a little, but he didn't respond at first. "We all work through things in our own way," he finally said.

* * * *

John had called Nancy that morning before he drove down to their house to visit her. As he'd expected, with the funeral over, most of their friends and extended family had gone back to their lives, leaving Nancy and the kids, except for her brother and his family, alone.

After visiting with them for about an hour, he'd hit his emotional limit and made excuses that he had to leave.

Working on George's enclosure without gloves, cutting the hardware cloth with tin snips and having the pokey ends scratching him, digging into his flesh, that'd been therapy. That it was helping Abbey made the pain so much sweeter.

I'll take my masochism where I can get it, any way I can get it.

And, obviously, she was happy with the results.

He knew George was. The tortoise had immediately started exploring as soon as he'd transferred him over to the new enclosure.

If anything he did made her not want to move out, he'd do it and keep doing it. Get her comfortable. Make her happy.

Serve her.

He suspected he was already well on the path to winning Tilly over. Once that happened, even Abbey wouldn't—he hoped—be able to refuse.

Even if all she did was live there and be his roommate, he'd be happy with that. Able to quietly serve her without her even realizing it.

Maybe, one day, something more could happen.

And if it didn't…

He didn't want to think like that yet. He darn sure wouldn't say it out loud for fear of coming off looking like a creepy guy.

At least George was happy. And seeing the smile on Abbey's face as she watched her beloved pet shamble around his new home would keep John satisfied for quite a while.

Chapter Thirteen

The Sunday before Abbey's surgery, there would be a Suncoast Society munch. Abbey had given serious thought about not going, but John talked her into it with logic, that it might be a while before she felt like going out once she had surgery. At least she didn't have to worry about Tom being there. He'd flown home that first weekend, texted her a thank-you for picking up his mail, and asked if she could pick it up again the next week, too.

Tilly told her to tell him to go to hell, but Abbey refused to be like that. She was determined to be the better person, completely at peace with how she'd handled herself and the situation.

This week, the munch was being held at Torino's. "I thought you didn't go to many of the munches," Abbey said to John.

"I don't, usually," he said. "But I'll go with you."

Not once in the nearly two weeks she'd lived with him had he been inappropriate. If anything, she felt bad that he wouldn't let her help out more with chores. He kept telling her once her back healed that she could pitch in, but he'd sic Tilly on her if he caught her overdoing it.

"I don't want you going if you don't want to go," she said.

"If you think I'm letting you drive all the way there alone, think again."

Her condition had deteriorated to the point that, for the past couple of days, Tilly had come over to drive her to and from work. Her last day of work had been Friday, and she'd spent most of Saturday either in bed, on the couch, or in the hot tub. John had become an expert at applying the leads for her TENS unit to her back, the only other thing that gave her any bit of pain relief besides the pain pills.

"I could call Tilly and see if they're going," she said.

He gave her "the look," as she was beginning to think of it. An arched eyebrow, the opposite corner of his mouth twisted in a scowl, his chin dipped as he stared at her. A look that meant he was done talking about it and had settled the issue in his mind. Usually the look he gave her when she tried to help clean up dishes or do other chores and he shut her down.

"No," he said. "I want to go, I'm taking you, and that's that."

"Yes, *sir*." She'd meant it sort of smartassedly, but it slipped from her mouth before she realized what she'd said.

He laughed. "Be careful how you say that around me." He walked over to where she sat on the couch and stared down at her. "Just because I've bottomed to you before doesn't mean I won't go all Dom on you to keep you in line until you've healed from your surgery. I'm a hell of a lot more scared by Tilly in her Domme mode than I am by you."

"Go all Dom on me, huh?"

"Yeah." He gave her "the look" again. "Ninety-five percent of my life is spent in a dominant headspace. I'm responsible for overseeing the health, welfare, and safety of hundreds of people in the course of my job. I'm no stranger to dealing with the press, attorneys, or upper management. You think I can't apply that same backbone to you and this situation, think again, *girl*."

Her throat went dry as she stared up into his eyes. Today, in this light, they looked a little more hazel than green, but they were intently focused on her.

She knew damn well he was joking around, but the thought seized her that, for once, it'd be nice to have someone to lean on in that way.

Especially when her upcoming surgery terrified the living fuck out of her.

She made a point of not blinking as she returned his gaze. "Yes,

Sir," she said again, more than a little amused to see the front of his shorts begin to tent.

* * * *

Oh...fuck.

John wanted to grab Abbey by the hair and drag her to bed and knew there were a bunch of reasons that couldn't happen, the first being her back injury, the second being they would need a long talk first.

But with that tone, and that look of playful defiance, and that damn, gorgeous pouty lip of hers, it didn't help that she was sitting at the perfect position he could shove his shorts down and—

Fuck, focus!

He knelt, grabbing her hands, eye to eye with her. "Abbey, I didn't mean you had to—"

"I know." She still returned his gaze with those gorgeous green eyes. "But you said you like to fix things, right? That it's your fetish?"

He nodded.

She squeezed his hands, hard. "I'm scared," she whispered. "Even if it's just between us for right now, until this is over...can I have *that*? It can be our secret. You don't have to tell anyone."

He had to think for a moment before it finally hit home what she was asking. She hadn't talked much about the surgery itself, even though he knew she wasn't looking forward to it. He sat on the couch next to her and put his arms around her, his cock now wilting as the full impact of just how terrified she really felt struck home.

"I'm scared about what's going to happen after," she whispered. "What if there's a problem? What if he sneezes while he's doing it and I'm in a wheelchair for the rest of my life? What if it doesn't fix my pain and I'm hurting this bad, or worse, for the rest of my life? Who will take care of George if something happens to me?"

He stroked her hair, his cheek pressed against her head, his eyes closed as he inhaled her scent and yet still tried to focus on what she was saying, to remain there for her.

"It's going to be okay," he said. "It's all right to be scared. I'd be nervous if I were going through it. I'm here for you, and I'm not going anywhere. I promise. However you need me."

He kissed the top of her head, lingering. "If that's what you need from me right now, I'm here for you. And no matter what, I promise I'll take care of George. That's one worry you don't need to have."

He felt her sobs before he heard them, her body trembling, then shaking as she tried to hold them back and couldn't. He suspected it was due in part to her nerves, and partially to the pain meds. He'd asked Tilly about it, noting a pattern of Abbey getting really emotional not long after taking a dose. Tilly had confirmed it was likely a side effect amplifying Abbey's frayed emotional state.

"Thank you, Sir," she whispered.

"Anything My girl wants or needs, that's what My girl gets," he softly said. It felt like the easiest designation, not sub, not slave, certainly no play would be happening right now. A term of endearment that didn't ask or promise more than either of them could deliver at that moment and didn't need any lengthy negotiations attached to it.

She took a deep breath and relaxed in his arms. "What time do you want to leave for dinner?" she asked in a voice that didn't sound much like the woman he'd come to know over the past couple of weeks. She sounded completely vulnerable in a way she hadn't before.

He cradled her chin in his palms, brushing her tears away with his thumbs. "We'll leave at six. I want you to wear something comfortable. And do *not* forget your cane, understand?"

She nodded. It was nearly impossible for her to stand up straight now without assistance. When she laid on the couch, she had to either be on her side with one knee drawn up, or if on her back, have several pillows under her knees to prop her legs up. He could only imagine the pain she was in.

When it came time to leave, he made her hang on to his arm and helped her out to the car, getting it started and letting it run with the AC on while he went back to lock the house and set the alarm. On the drive there, she rested her hand on his thigh, a sweet, nearly painful distraction as his throbbing cock got uncomfortably pinched by his jeans.

He wouldn't adjust himself though, not a fan of CBT usually, but the pain a welcomed distraction nonetheless.

There were a few familiar cars in the restaurant's parking lot when they arrived. "So here's how we'll handle tonight," he said. "I don't want you discussing things that will upset you. All you have to say about Tom is that you're no longer together, he took a job out of state, and that you're living with me now."

He was all too aware of a couple of single "do-me" male submissives that frequently attended the munches. He'd heard Tilly talking about them. How they would swoop in and try to pester single female Dominants for attention.

"Tonight," he continued, "you stay on my arm, and let people make whatever assumptions they want to make. If anyone bugs you, I'll take care of them for you. Understand?"

She smiled. It was an increasingly rare sight lately as her pain levels climbed. "Yes, Sir. What about the introductions?"

"We just say our names. Tony's running it tonight. I'll ask him not to give us a hard time."

He started to unfasten his seat belt when she reached out and stayed his hand. "Thank you, John," she said.

Those three words, from her, filled him like cool water on a parched afternoon.

He leaned in and brushed a kiss across her lips. "You're very welcome, Ab," he said. Then he waggled his eyebrows at her to lighten the mood. "Thank *you* for willingly letting me indulge in *my* fetish."

A slightly wider smile from her that time.

He'd consider it a win.

* * * *

Tilly and her guys showed up a few minutes after their arrival. John had seated Abbey at a table and went to speak with Tony, but then intercepted Tilly and had a quick word with her, too. She nodded and made a beeline for Abbey, settling in on her other side.

"So what are you two planning, huh?" Abbey asked.

Tilly smiled. "Noneyo."

Abbey rolled her eyes. "Is *too* my business, when it's me y'all are plotting against."

"They're not plotting against you, Abbey," Cris said from Landry's other side. "But you are outnumbered."

John returned from talking with Tony. "He knows not to give us a hard time. He'll call on me first, then you, then Tilly. That way we can get our intros done first and fast and it won't look weird."

"Oh, *great*," Tilly joked. "Sure, throw *me* on the sword." Her smile belied her words.

"Take one for the team, love," Landry joked.

Despite needing another pain pill toward the end of dinner, Abbey was glad John had talked her into coming. He and Tilly together fended off an annoying single submissive guy who was new and didn't realize what a tool he was being toward Abbey. Normally, she would have no problem shutting down someone like that, but tonight it just wasn't in her.

There was no fight, no strength. Every ounce of will she had was focused on trying to hang on until her surgery.

I just need to make it through Wednesday.

She felt like a wuss about that. She darn well knew there were people out there in chronic pain far worse than what she was going through, who lived with it. Normally she wasn't someone to knuckle under when it came to pain. This level of pain, however, was a totally alien feeling. Like someone had stuck a sharp filet knife into her spine and was forcibly turning it every couple of hours. A pain that didn't fade, that only got worse.

When they returned home, it was still early, but she didn't want to go to bed yet.

John, however, apparently saw right through her.

"We need to get you comfortable," he said.

"I'm going to be stuck by myself for a couple of weeks," she said, trying not to pout. "I want company while I can have it."

"Then we'll settle you into your bed and I'll come in there and watch TV with you. Deal?"

Incredibly simple. And it would give her a guilt-free way of snuggling with him. She did miss that about Tom, missed human contact.

Missed having another body sleeping in bed with her.

"Okay. Deal."

He helped her into her room, then went to check on George. With everything fine in Tortoise Town, John changed into a pair of shorts and joined her in bed with his own pillow.

As she was trying to find a comfortable position, he said, "Hey, I just had a really stupid thought."

"What?"

"We need to put you in my bedroom after your surgery. My bathroom will be easier for you to move around in. And I have the shower stall in there. In your bathroom, you have to step over the side of the tub. I don't want you falling."

She knew, logically, where he was going with this.

She also saw her perfect opening. "I'd feel weird sleeping in there, alone in a strange bed." She finally took a chance and met his gaze.

His eyes were focused straight into hers, as if trying to decipher her meaning.

He slowly nodded. "Okay, then. Would you feel better if I slept in there with you?"

She nodded.

He arched an eyebrow at her again. Despite her pain, her clit thrummed a little. There was just something about the way he did that.

When she was back up to full strength, if he wanted to be more than just friends, she was going to give the man a ride for his money's worth.

"Would you like me to sleep in here with you tonight?" he asked.

She nodded. "Yes, Sir," she whispered.

And now that sexy little half smile thing he did.

He laid down next to her. "You understand the risk here, right? You might wake up and find a woody poking against you."

"I'm willing to help you with that, if you want me to."

The act dropped as he sat up again. "Abbey, no. Not that I don't appreciate the offer," he quickly added, "because I do and, believe me, under different circumstances I'd be more than happy to take you up on it. It's okay to joke around right now, but I know you're in a lot of pain. This isn't about me. Seriously."

He laced his fingers through hers. "Hey, I'll consider it a form of masochism, okay? I'll also lay it on the table that once you're feeling better, if you want to have some discussions about this, I'm good with that, too. For right now, my focus is on you, on getting you through Wednesday and healed up. Got it?" He brought her hand to his lips and kissed it.

"Promise?"

He looked a little confused. "Promise what?"

"Once we're through this, that we'll talk."

His expression softened. "Yes. After. You've been through an emotional meat grinder, and you're in a lot of pain. Personally, I would feel like I'm taking advantage of you. I'm not going anywhere. This discussion can wait." He smiled. "Frankly, I think George could outrun you at this point, so it's not like I'm worried about you running off anywhere."

"Yeah. No shit."

He settled in next to her, on his side, his body pressed against her back, the warmth from him washing through her T-shirt and into her flesh.

It felt even better when he draped his arm around her waist and she was able to lace fingers with him. Like that, she immediately dropped off to sleep.

* * * *

John lay there long after the sound of her breathing slowed and deepened and he knew she was asleep. He'd taken off the next two weeks, using vacation time.

Which was a good thing, because tonight, lying next to her like this, with her in his arms, he knew he wouldn't get much sleep.

And not just because of his cock, which seemed to fit perfectly along the seam of her ass, his shorts and her panties the only barrier between them.

Torture.

Not even good torture, because he realized how much pain she was in. He couldn't enjoy that.

He wasn't glad that she was in agony. Not a bit. The bad kind of pain had taken its toll on her. He had friends who'd gone through similar surgeries and basically gotten their lives back after.

But he wouldn't deny he felt glad that Tom had been an idiot. Because now John knew he had his own chance at happiness with Abbey, as long as he didn't do anything stupid to fuck it up.

And as long as she still wanted him when she was recovered. Once she was no longer dependent upon him, once she was feeling back to her old self, that would be the test.

All he could do now was take it one day at a time.

Chapter Fourteen

Abbey was already awake when John lightly tapped on her shoulder Wednesday morning.

"I'm awake."

"You ready?"

"No. But I know it has to be done. I can't put it off."

He carefully got up without jostling her and walked around to the other side of the bed. There, he reached for her hand. "I promise you, I'll be there. So will Tilly, Cris, and Landry. We're all going to be out there waiting for you."

She somehow managed to hold the tears back. "Will you please go into pre-op with me?"

He nodded. "Of course. You don't want Tilly?"

"Only if they'll let me have a second person." She finally found the courage to ask it. "Can we tell them you're my fiancé or something today? So they don't try to keep you out?" She hadn't told her family the details about her surgery, not wanting them there and crowding around her and squabbling with each other when she didn't have energy to deal with them. She'd told them she would be having surgery soon, but hadn't given them the date or invited them to be there.

If something bad happened, John had their information and had promised Abbey he'd notify them, even as he forcefully reminded her, yet again, that she likely would come through the surgery just fine.

"We'll tell them anything you want." He kissed her hand, holding it against his chest. "Whatever you want."

"I'm scared."

"I know you are. I know this is scary. But your surgeon is good and there's no reason to think you'll have anything but a normal surgery and recovery. Remember what Tilly told you, focus on the finish line. This should put an end to your pain once you heal up. You'll have your life back."

"Will you please come into the recovery room with me? I don't want to be in there alone and unconscious. Please?"

While she knew it was rare, she'd heard horror stories about unconscious female patients being molested. Yes, it was as irrational a fear as her fear of spiders, but it was still a fear.

"I don't know if they'll let me."

"Tilly will get you in there."

"You know, she probably can. I'll promise to try. I don't want to get tossed out of the hospital."

"Okay."

He helped her stand. Considering how bad her pain had grown lately, she knew this had to be done. If her condition deteriorated, she'd get to a point where she wouldn't be able to walk.

He helped her into the bathroom. He stepped out while she used the toilet, then returned, helping her get her T-shirt off and offering a steadying arm to her as she got into the shower. She had to use the special antiseptic soap again and was grateful when John reached in, took the washcloth from her, and gently scrubbed her back for her.

She didn't care if he saw her totally naked. They'd crossed that line a long time ago. It was more humiliating for her that she felt nearly helpless and had to rely on him when he already had so much going on in his life. Even though he proclaimed he was happy to help, it still grated on her that she needed the help in the first place. That life and circumstances had robbed her of the freedom to choose whether or not to accept his help.

That was what she hated.

He helped her get dressed and waited while she brushed her teeth.

Then he brushed her hair for her, pulling it back into a ponytail.

When she met his gaze in the mirror, he offered her a smile. "I promise," he said, "I'll be there."

"You won't run off to Dallas?" she whispered.

"No. Never. I'll never abandon you."

She turned and hugged him. That was when she realized what she wasn't smelling. "You didn't make coffee?"

He looked confused. "No. Why?"

"But...coffee."

"You can't have coffee."

"But *you* can."

"I'm not having anything to eat until after we get you there and you're in. Tilly or Cris or Landry can run get me something while we're waiting."

"But that's not fair to you."

"Life's not fair." He gently cupped her face in his hand. "Can I ask you a favor?"

She nodded.

"For today, shift your brain out of control mode and let me take care of you without you second-guessing or feeling guilty about it. Okay? Do you trust me enough to let me do that for you?"

Of course she did. "Yeah. Thank you."

With his arm firmly around her waist, he helped her out to the sofa to wait while he finished getting ready. She realized he must have already taken care of George, because the blinds out to the lanai were pulled open a little.

He really was taking care of her. Not just her, but George, too.

As she sat there and looked around, it hit her just how many of her things he'd incorporated into his home over the past couple of weeks. Some of her family pictures sat on a shelf next to a few of his. Several of her turtle and tortoise figurines were interspersed on the top of the entertainment center with things he'd collected on various vacations, like a ceramic lighthouse from Michigan and a small model of the St.

Louis Arch.

I'm home.

Not once had he made mention of her moving out. Not even when she'd made hypothetical statements about needing to start looking at apartments had he ever talked about her moving.

It was like he'd gone out of his way to steer the conversation in a different direction.

And then there was Tortoise Town.

Maybe she was engaging in wishful thinking. She didn't trust herself anymore. Not when she looked back on her relationship with Tom. Maybe she was doing something similar now, seeing what she wanted to see instead of the full truth.

Maybe I need Tilly to reality-check me.

For now, it was a topic she'd have to shelve until she was through this.

* * * *

Tilly and her guys met them at the hospital. The nurse let John stay with Abbey while she changed into her hospital gown and while they started her IV. Only then was Tilly allowed to come back and join them.

For simplicity's sake, on the hospital paperwork she designated John as her fiancé and next of kin, and Tilly as her sister. That way they both could access her records and receive information. She certainly felt closer to them than her blood kin. Not that she didn't love her family, but as stressed as she felt today, she refused to add to it. Today, she would let John and Tilly supervise her care as much as they could.

When the anesthesiologist came back to talk to her, Tilly took over and asked for a dose of Versed to relax Abbey.

"What's that?" Abbey asked, her fingers tightly clamped around John's hand.

Tilly laughed. "Something to keep the circulation going in his fingers," she said as she nodded toward John's hand. "It'll relax you."

The doctor returned a few minutes later and added the dose to Abbey's IV. Within a minute, Abbey felt the world soften around her, the anxiety melting away.

"Aaand there she goes," Tilly said, smiling.

Abbey looked at John. "Don't leave me alone in recovery," she said. "Please."

"Honey," Tilly said, "we'll do our best. Don't worry, there are plenty of nurses in there. No one's going to do anything bad to you."

Two nurses came for Abbey. "It's time."

Abbey pulled John close, kissing him. "I love you, Sir," she whispered.

He smiled, stroking her forehead. "Love you, too, sweetheart," he whispered back. "You go to sleep and when you wake up, you'll be on the road to feeling better."

Tilly gave her a kiss on the cheek, and then she was being wheeled away.

As the anesthesiologist slipped a mask over her face, he looked down at her over the top of his surgical mask. "Just take deep breaths and count back for me…"

* * * *

Tilly stood there with John, watching as they wheeled Abbey down the hall.

She gently rested a hand on his shoulder. "I heard that," she said.

When he looked, he saw she wore a smirk. "What?"

"The 'Sir.' And the 'I love yous.'"

"So?"

He thought Tilly was going to bust his balls over it, but she shocked him.

She pulled him in for a hug.

"Promise me," she whispered. "Promise me you won't fuck things up with her. You won't hurt her."

"I won't. I promise."

She finally let him go. "Good. Now, let's go get you something to eat. I bet you didn't even have coffee yet, did you?"

"No." He followed her out to the waiting room. "How'd you know?"

Tilly turned, smiling at him. "Because you're a good egg, even if you are a little cracked."

* * * *

Abbey had proven feistier than her recovery nurses anticipated. When John and Tilly were called back from the waiting room by a nurse, she arched an eyebrow at them.

"Don't know how she is normally," the nurse said, "but apparently she's used to getting her way. She says she won't calm down unless we bring you two back."

Tilly grinned and elbowed John. "Knew she'd pitch a fit."

Abbey lay propped on her side with pillows, a nurse sitting on a rolling chair next to her bed and filling out a report.

"Here's her fiancé and sister," the other nurse said.

"Good. Her numbers were getting a little sketchy."

John leaned in and kissed Abbey. She opened her eyes long enough to see it was him before they dropped closed again and she blindly groped for his hand.

"You settle down now," he softly said. "Don't cause trouble."

She squeezed his hand long and hard, desperately. He understood her fear, even if he didn't share it. And if she needed him to stand there all afternoon next to her, and if the staff allowed it, he would.

"Abbey," Tilly said, "you're fine. You'll be moved to a room once they're satisfied you're doing okay."

"Actually," the nurse with the chart said, "it might be a little longer than that. They're full upstairs. Right now, they don't have a room for her. That's the other reason we're bending the rules a little for her. It might be several hours before we can get her upstairs."

They brought chairs for John and Tilly. It was actually after six o'clock by the time they had a room ready for Abbey. On the way upstairs, they collected Landry and Cris. They offered to stay with Abbey while John ran home to check on George and take care of him.

As he drove, relief filled him. Abbey had come through the surgery all right. If her feistiness post-op was any indication, she'd be okay.

When he returned to the hospital, he brought an overnight bag with him. Their private rooms allowed patients to have someone stay with them, if they chose.

After Tilly and the others left for the night and John settled in, Abbey spoke up.

"Sir?"

He got up and went to her side. "I'm right here."

She looked like she was in a lot of pain. He reached over and hit the button on her morphine pump, the beep indicating it had delivered a dose.

"Thank you for staying with me."

"Sweetheart, I told you, I'm here for you."

"You don't have to spend the night if you don't want to."

"I want to."

"Really?"

"Yeah, really."

"Okay."

And with that, she drifted off again.

He stared down at her, watching her sleep.

Now, with this over and her healing able to start, maybe he could truly begin to show her just how much he wanted to be there for her.

For the rest of their lives, if she'd let him.

* * * *

Abbey was sitting up in bed after having kept her breakfast down. Everything hurt.

John, with the assistance of the nurse, had helped Abbey out of bed and into the bathroom when she refused to use a bed pan in the middle of the night. When the doctor showed up for morning rounds with his PA in tow, he smiled as he glanced over her chart on the rolling computer terminal.

"How do you feel about going home today?" the doctor asked.

"What?"

John frowned as he looked up from his work laptop, where he was dealing with e-mails. "You're releasing her the next day?" They'd originally told Abbey she might be in two or three days, depending on how she healed.

"The nurses say she ate her breakfast, and she was up and walking last night."

"Yeah, but—"

"I can go home?" Abbey asked.

"No reason not to send you home," the doctor said.

"I thought people usually had to be in for a couple of days after this kind of surgery," John said, suspecting insurance-mandated fuckery afoot.

"Well, sure, a few years ago. Not anymore. Surgical techniques have improved. If a patient is eating and has help at home, no reason not to send them home. Her records indicate you're her caregiver, correct?"

"Yeah, but—"

"I want to go home," Abbey said.

John wanted to argue with her, but knew if the doctor wanted to discharge her and Abbey wanted to be discharged, likely he couldn't fight it either way. "Okay."

"I'll write her orders and we'll have her come in to my office on

Monday for a check."

"Thank you, doctor," Abbey said.

John immediately called Tilly.

"What the *hell*? What do you mean they're discharging her? No, she should stay at least another day."

"Then you get your ass down here and help me," he said, trying to keep Abbey from overhearing him where he stood by the window. "She wants to go home."

"Shit. I'll be right there."

When Tilly showed up thirty minutes later, she couldn't dissuade the doctor or Abbey.

Tilly pulled John out into the hall to talk. "Probably the goddamned insurance," she said. "They shuttle people out as fast as they can to save money. That, and they're full up and trying to clear beds."

"What do we do?"

"We take her home. I suspect come tomorrow morning she's going to wish she still had that morphine pump. Unless she asks to be kept in and is complaining of pain, she's out the door."

* * * *

John was less than happy about the discharge, but Tilly stayed with them, helping him get Abbey dressed and into the wheelchair a nurse brought for her. Tilly waited with Abbey by the front door while John went to get his car.

They had to pick up prescriptions for her on the way home. Tilly followed them, helping John get Abbey out of the car and into bed.

"I'll come by at six to check on her," Tilly said as John walked her out.

"Thanks."

She gave him another hug at the front door. "Thank you."

With that, she left.

He closed the door behind her. If he'd managed to get onto Tilly's good side, he wouldn't do anything to fuck that up.

After Tilly left following the six o'clock check on her, Abbey wanted to move out to the couch.

"Why?"

"Because I want to see George. Bring him in and let him wander around the living room, please."

John got her situated and comfortable on the couch, the TV remote on the coffee table where she could easily reach it without stretching, ditto a bottle of water. After bringing George in and putting him on the floor where she could see him, a few pieces of romaine in front of him to keep the tortoise there and busy, John settled onto the floor next to the couch.

"You don't have to sit down there," she said, her voice sounding weak and pained and still a little hoarse from the surgery.

"I know I don't," he said. "But this way we can talk without having to ask each other to repeat what we just said." He offered her a smile he hoped hid his thoughts and feelings. He didn't want her stressed out by his issues, didn't want her to feel any pressure.

That was the last thing he wanted to do to her. He wanted her to relax, to heal, to let go and let him handle things. It wasn't a case of her having to be a Dominant, or being dominant in any form. It was a matter of him wanting to serve her, take care of her. If someone else wanted to call that submissive, well, it didn't matter.

"That's not going to be very comfortable for you," she said.

"Comfort is a relative term. Remember, I'll take my masochism however I can get it."

He leaned his back against the couch, well aware of her presence inches from him.

As the movie started, she rested one hand on his shoulder. "Thank you for everything you've done for me. I can't begin to tell you how much I appreciate it. I meant what I said. I love you."

He turned his head so he could kiss the back of her hand. Then he placed his hand on top of hers, tipping his head to the side to rest his cheek against her arm. "I love you, too."

Closing his eyes, he listened to the movie, not really caring about it.

He could sit here all night, even if she was asleep and the TV turned off, just to be here, to be helpful. Appreciated.

No stranger to play or pain, he couldn't remember anything that had ever left him feeling as fulfilled and satisfied as he did at that moment.

He waited until nearly midnight to corral George, making sure to wipe up the floor and wash his hands thoroughly before waking Abbey to move her back to the bedroom. After helping her to the bathroom, he got her situated in bed, on her side so he could spoon against her.

She laced her fingers through his. "Thank you, Sir," she sleepily said. He wasn't sure how awake she really was, the pain killers no doubt still hitting her heavy.

He kissed the nape of her neck. "Sweet dreams, My beautiful girl," he whispered.

Closing his eyes, he knew he, for one, would sleep well that night.

Chapter Fifteen

The next morning, John prepared Abbey's meds and her breakfast before he took it in to her. He knelt next to her side of the bed, watching her sleep and grateful for the opportunity to be there for her.

"Good morning, sweetheart."

She mumbled at him.

"Time to wake up."

She finally opened her eyes. "I don't feel good."

"I know, sweetie. I have your meds, and some breakfast. You need to take them or I'll call Tilly."

"That's playing dirty."

"I know, sweetheart. I'm sorry."

He helped her sit up, freezing in place while she breathed through the pain before she gave him a nod to keep going. Once she was on her feet, he helped her into the bathroom, staying with her while she took care of things and washed her hands before she headed back to bed.

With her sitting on the edge of the bed, and him standing there, his leg braced against the edge of the bed for her to hold onto if she lost her balance, he got her to take her medicine—antibiotics and painkillers—and swallow them down with some orange juice. She ate a whole container of yogurt for him before he helped her back into bed.

He turned the TV on, but she was already asleep in less than ten minutes. So he grabbed his laptop and work phone and started combing through his work e-mail. Tilly would come over later in the morning to check on her. George could wait for his morning cleaning until then. John didn't want to leave Abbey alone if he didn't have to, not her first morning back home.

He had to wake her up at lunchtime for her to take her next round of meds, and to eat something. Tilly had already come and gone without Abbey waking up.

John worried about that, about how much Abbey was sleeping. Tilly assured him that since it was her first full day home, she likely would sleep. Catching up from the hospital, in addition to the pain meds.

But by that evening, it was even harder for him to wake Abbey for dinner and her medication.

"I don't feel good," she said after he got her to the bathroom and back to bed.

She didn't look good, either. Relatively speaking. And her skin felt a little warm, even though the thermostat was turned down and the house felt comfortable to him. "Do you want me to call Tilly?"

"No. When is my doctor appointment Monday?"

"Ten."

"Okay."

She would only eat a few bites of her dinner. Then she went straight back to sleep.

By ten o'clock, he reached over and laid the back of his hand against her forehead. She felt like a blast furnace. He gently stroked her shoulder, trying to wake her. "Abbey, do you want something to drink?"

She didn't stir at first. He tried again. When she woke up and tried to get up by herself, he hurried over to her side of the bed.

"I feel sick," she said. Her voice sounded slurred, thick.

He had just enough time to grab the garbage can from next to the bed before she threw up. After she'd emptied what little was in her stomach, he got a wet washcloth and cup of water for her, but he didn't like how hot she felt. "I'm calling Tilly."

"No, I'm okay," she weakly said.

"You're *not* okay." He reached across the bed and grabbed his phone.

Tilly arrived ten minutes later, complete with a bag of gear. When she felt Abbey's forehead with the back of her hand, she shot John a glare. "How long's she been running a fever?" She dug a digital thermometer out of her bag and pressed it against Abbey's ear.

"She's been warm for a while."

The thermometer beeped, Tilly's face going flat when she read it. After taking Abbey's pulse and blood pressure and listening to her heart, breath, and bowel sounds with a stethoscope, Tilly said, "Abbey, sweetie, I need to look at your back."

"The doctor said not to take the dressing off."

"I know, honey. I'm not going to. I just need to look."

John helped get Abbey into position. When Tilly lifted Abbey's T-shirt and peeked down the top of the bandage, using a penlight to see underneath it, John didn't like the expression that crossed her face.

"Okay, that's real good, sweetie. I need to make a phone call." She bolted off the bed, her cell phone in hand as she headed for the hall.

John raced after her once he was sure Abbey was comfortable. He reached the living room in time to hear Tilly apparently talking to an ambulance dispatcher and giving them John's address.

"What the—"

Tilly held up a hand to silence him until she finished the call. "Go get dressed, and get your shit ready. Get her purse and wallet and stuff. The ambulance will be here in about five minutes. You're riding with her."

"But—"

"She's got an infection. There's something seriously wrong, and we need to get her to the hospital right now. I'll lock the house up and follow you there with Cris and Landry. Go!"

He went, changing clothes and grabbing stuff, ready just as he heard the ambulance pull up in front of the house. He assumed Tilly would let them in, and she did. He was waiting and ready in the bedroom when the crew brought a gurney in, following Tilly to the master bedroom.

Helpless, John stood back and watched while Tilly and the paramedics got Abbey positioned and transferred to the gurney.

"What's going on?" Abbey weakly asked.

He felt like he'd failed her. He had one job, one goddamned job, to take care of her, and he'd fucked that up miserably.

"Honey," Tilly said, "you've got an infection. We're going to get you back to the hospital right now and they're going to get you some better medicine. Probably IV."

"But...drive me."

"We don't want to put the pressure on your back. Let these hunks load you up and carry your ass."

"John—"

"Is going with you. He's right here and he'll be with you."

Another paramedic walked in with a clipboard, taking notes as Tilly gave him Abbey's vitals and the details about what she suspected.

He turned to John. "And you are, sir?"

"Her boyfriend," Tilly said, meeting John's gaze. "He's riding with you to the hospital."

* * * *

Everything happened in a blur from that point. John was sitting in the ER waiting room, where a nurse had parked him, when Tilly and her guys arrived fifteen minutes later.

"Where is she?" Tilly asked.

"They said they had to take her back for treatment," he said.

"But they put her in an ER bed, right?"

"They moved her." It had all happened so fast, he was trying to process it. A doctor on duty had been immediately summoned when a nurse carefully peeled up a corner of Abbey's surgical dressing and looked at it. "They said they'd come get me."

They'd rushed Abbey out of the room on a gurney, looks of professional concern on their faces, expressions he knew couldn't bode well.

That wasn't good enough for Tilly. She marched up to the desk. "I need to check on a patient. Abbegail Rockland. I'm her sister…"

He tuned it out.

Tilly returned a minute later looking stunned.

"What?" he asked.

"They didn't take her for treatment. They took her back for emergency surgery."

* * * *

Five minutes later a surgical nurse came for them, leading them to the surgical waiting area. The short version was it looked like Abbey's incision had either ripped open, or the infection had caused it to open, they didn't know. They'd had to get Abbey into surgery immediately, to clean out and close the wound, and get her pumped full of heavy-duty antibiotics to kill whatever was causing the infection.

John sat there feeling worthless, useless. "I failed her," he said.

Tilly slung an arm around his shoulders. "Hey, stop that. I was there earlier today. I thought she felt a little warm, but I didn't take her temp. I should have. I'm the nurse, not you. It's not your fault."

"I should have called you sooner. All day she said she hasn't felt well."

"Yeah, well, she'd just had surgery. Hey, Sir Fussypants here popped a blood vessel and vomited blood and scared the crap out of me and Cris. Shit happens. Even when you do everything right. And you did everything right."

"I wish you wouldn't call me that," Landry said.

"If the shoe fits," Tilly shot back.

"If I *had* done everything right," John said, "she wouldn't be in surgery again."

"Cris, help me out," Tilly said.

"She's right. As an experienced caregiver, trust me when I say you can't prepare for everything."

"If *I'm* not blaming you," Tilly said, "then you can't blame yourself. The incision could have ripped open when she vomited from the infection. Or it could have been the source of the infection. Until the doctor tells us what's going on, it's all conjecture and you can stop beating yourself up over it."

"How'd you feel when Landry got sick?"

"Apples and hand grenades," she immediately countered. "Besides, we're talking about you, not me. If you *want* me to beat you up, I will. Later. For now, stay focused on her. Hell, if the stupid insurance company hadn't dictated only a one-day stay in the hospital, maybe they would have caught this. If anyone's to blame, it's the goddamned bean counters."

It was another hour before they got an update. Abbey's blood pressure had plummeted during the procedure, but they got it back up after pumping more fluids into her. They'd be closing her incision shortly and she'd go straight into surgical ICU.

"What kind of infection is it?" Tilly asked. "And what caused it?"

"We're still waiting on blood work to come back," the weary-looking nurse said. "As soon as we know, we'll pass it along."

"I'm guessing they won't kick her out the door again tomorrow," John bitterly said.

Tilly patted him on the back. "Not if we have anything to say about it."

It was nearly five a.m. before they allowed John and Tilly back into the ICU to see Abbey. She was still sedated and would likely not be conscious until later that morning. They'd isolated the type of infection she had and adjusted her IV meds accordingly.

Now, it was just wait and see.

When John said he'd wait in the waiting room, Tilly, with the help of Landry and Cris, overruled him and steered him out to their car.

"It's no use for you to stay here right now," Tilly said. "You need sleep. She'd want you to get some sleep. The staff said they'd call you if there were any changes."

"I need to call her family."

"Nope. Not yet," Tilly said. "You know how she feels about that. The last thing she needs is the aggravation of them swooping in and bugging the crap out of her and squabbling with each other in the process. I'm sure she'll be conscious later today and she'll tell us what she wants us to do."

* * * *

Abbey felt like she was caught in a nightmare she couldn't escape. That she was being tortured. Beeps, noises, people moving her, and searing pain from her back, worse than anything before.

John.

She wanted to cry out for him, reach out to him, but the world went dark.

When she finally forced her eyes open again, she wasn't home, in their bed. The walls couldn't be anything but a hospital room.

It took too much energy to keep her eyes open, so she closed them and tried to speak. Even her throat hurt, worse than it had before.

"Sir." She said it blindly, praying he was there, somewhere. That she wasn't alone.

A hand laced fingers with her, warm, comforting, gently squeezing. "I'm right here," he said.

Tears slipped down her cheeks as he stroked her forehead.

"What happened?" Speaking was agony, shards of glass grinding along her windpipe.

"You're in the surgical ICU. You got an infection. Your incision opened up. They had to close it and pump you full of antibiotics." She felt him brush the tears from her cheeks before his hand rested on top of her head again, gently stroking her hair.

She squeezed the hand holding his. "Please take me home, Sir."

"Sweetheart, I can't. You have to stay here until your body fights off the infection."

She heard a strange woman's voice, speaking to John. Felt someone touch her left arm, taking her pulse. A blood pressure cuff squeezed her upper left arm, then the other presence faded.

Abbey tried again to open her eyes and found herself staring into John's face. His expression looked haggard, drawn.

Scared.

Her eyes fell closed again. She also noted it looked like he hadn't shaved in a couple of days, which couldn't be right. "What day is it?"

"It's Sunday morning, sweetheart. Do you remember the ambulance ride Friday night?"

She remembered…something. But it was all a pain-filled blur. "Tilly?"

"She'll be back in a little while. They don't want a lot of people in here at the same time. Your last blood work showed you're improving. They might move you to a regular room tonight. Then I can stay with you."

She heard someone else enter the room again. "Ms. Rockland? I'm Dr. Kaulfell. Can you tell me what your pain level is?"

"Bad."

"Okay. Now that you're awake, we're going to get you a pump for your pain. You can hit the button when you need it. For now, I'll have the nurses give you another dose to make you comfortable."

John squeezed her hand. "Sweetheart, I have to go back out to the waiting room."

One more time, she forced her eyes open. "Please don't leave me."

He rested his head on the bed, his forehead touching hers. "I'll *never* leave you. I promise. But I have to follow the rules or they won't let me back in here." He lowered his voice. "We're already pushing it telling them Tilly is your sister."

"Please, don't call my family."

"We haven't. Tilly texted them from your phone and pretended to be you and said you needed to rest. Your mom's sick with a cold anyway, so it's moot. She's told them next week, when you're back home, you'll call them."

Her eyes fell closed again. "Thank you."

A nurse came in and gave her a dose of pain meds through her IV. John leaned in and kissed Abbey's forehead.

"Go to sleep, sweetheart. You're safe here. You just get better."

She fell back into the void of her nightmares.

Chapter Sixteen

Abbey awoke to the feeling that the world was moving, spinning. When she forced her eyes open, she saw it was. More accurately, she realized her bed was moving, turning. She closed her eyes when vertigo tied to take over.

"Abbey," a woman said, "you're being moved out of ICU to a room."

"Sir," she whispered.

"I'm right here, sweetheart," John said from what sounded like somewhere behind her head. "Tilly and the others are waiting right outside."

Relief filled her. She wasn't alone.

Someone put something small, round, and hard in her hand. "That's the control for your morphine pump," the woman said. "Your thumb is on the button. When you're in pain, push that. It can't give you more than it's programmed for, so push it as much as you need to."

Abbey pushed it and heard a long beep.

"There you go."

She kept her eyes closed, her teeth gritted against the small bumps and jolts as they rolled her out of the ICU and down hallways, through doors, into and out of an elevator, and then, finally, into a room.

She tried to push the button again, but this time it didn't beep.

At least the pain had subsided a little, not nearly as excruciating as it had felt the last time she'd been aware of it.

She heard nurses talking, and Tilly's voice, too, discussing her chart and condition. Finally, the sound of a door shutting, muffling noises from the hall.

"Sir?" she whispered.

"Right here, sweetheart. Tilly, Landry, and Cris are here, too." His hand engulfed hers.

It was a little easier to open her eyes this time and keep them open. At least John had shaved at some point.

She reached up and stroked his chin. "Did you sleep?"

"Don't worry about me."

The door opened again, Tilly's voice filling the room. "They said she can have little sips of water. I brought her some."

She walked around the bed and handed John the cup with the straw. He held it to Abbey's lips and she took a sip. It hurt going down, but the cool water felt good in her parched mouth.

"Here," Tilly said, pulling a tube of lip balm from her pocket. "I just bought it downstairs." She unwrapped it and handed it to John. He swapped the cup for the tube of lip balm and coated Abbey's lips with it.

"Can you stay?" Abbey asked him.

He nodded. "I'm sleeping here tonight with you."

Relief filled her. "What time is it?"

"It's a little after six o'clock Sunday evening."

Holy crap. A whole weekend lost.

"What happened?"

Tilly filled her in. "Long story short, you're lucky John was paying attention and called me Friday night. If he'd waited until morning, they might not have been able to pull you back." Her expression looked grim. "I feel responsible for not taking your temperature Friday morning when I stopped by. I would have had him drive you to the doctor then and they would have caught it sooner."

The lip balm tasted vaguely like cherry and helped soothe her chapped lips a little. "You can't kill him." Abbey managed what she hoped looked like a smile.

Tilly laughed. "Hell, no, I'm not killing him. He's taking care of my bestie. Don't worry, he's safe." She patted him on the shoulder. "Doesn't mean once you're feeling better that I might not beg you to let me go after him from time to time, but he's family now. He's earned immunity from outright murder by me."

Abbey squeezed John's hand. "He certainly has."

* * * *

They kept Abbey in the hospital for another three days before discharging her this time. With orders from both John and Tilly not to rush it, and not wanting a repeat of the problem, Abbey didn't fight them or push to go home sooner.

That night, Abbey lay snuggled against John in their bed, finally able to relax for the first time since the nightmare started. No alarms to startle her out of a sound sleep, no people leaning over her to take her vitals in the middle of the night and scaring her, no worrying about her safety or privacy.

It felt good to be home, with John.

The next morning when she awoke, he was waiting and ready to help her up and out of bed and to the bathroom.

"Can I take a shower?"

"We can't get your dressing wet. Tilly loaned me a shower chair they used for Landry. You can have a sponge bath."

Ick. She was sick of sponge baths and wanted a real one. She decided to push a little. She felt drastically different now than she had the first time around following her initial surgery and knew she was healing.

After the brush she'd had with Fate, she didn't want to dick around and delay things with John any longer.

"I can't even shave my own legs right now," she said. "Will you please help me? I want more than just a sponge bath. I want to wash my hair, too. The shower's big enough for both of us." She opted to play dirty. "Please, Sir?"

There went the eyebrow. "Why do I get the distinct impression you're up to something?"

"Please?" She fought the urge to hold her breath.

"Okay. Just, please, stop looking so pitiful. That's not fair."

"Thank you."

"I'll get my bathing suit."

"Why?"

Another arched eyebrow. "*Why*? Seriously?"

"I don't mind," she said. "I'll be naked. You've been seeing me naked in the hospital."

"Abbey, you're still recovering. Are you really sure this is a conversation you want to—"

"Please?"

"No more pouty lip."

She clamped her lips together.

That made him laugh, the smile a welcomed sight on his handsome face when he'd looked worried for too long. "Okay, but I apologize in advance for any inappropriateness on the part of my cock. It's got a mind of its own, ya know."

That was what she was hoping, but she wouldn't admit it. If she admitted it, he would overrule her and put the kibosh on her whole plan. "No problem."

He got her into the shower and seated on the shower chair. Then he disappeared for a minute and returned with a rain poncho. "We'll wash your hair first," he said, helping her put it on and tucking a towel around the inside of the neck opening to keep water out. "Then I'll shave your legs for you."

"Thank you."

She watched as he stripped off his T-shirt, shorts, and briefs and stepped inside the shower with her.

Oh...my.

The man was hung.

She closed her eyes as he used the handheld shower massage head to wash her hair, having her hold it between rinses, when he needed both hands. His fingers massaging her scalp felt goood.

When he finished that, he wrapped her hair in another towel on top of her head and carefully got the poncho off her without dislodging that towel. He had her hold the showerhead again while he knelt in front of her and started lathering her left leg with shaving gel.

Despite her pain, her clit throbbed. She knew she was wet, and knew there wasn't really a damn thing she could do about it right then, but she didn't even care.

This was the closest she'd gotten to sex since she got hurt, and she wasn't about to let him stop.

She didn't miss, despite his attempt to hide it from her, that his cock had hardened.

He tried to stop shaving her leg at the knee, but she scooted forward as far as she could on the shower chair without overbalancing. "No," she softly said. "Farther." She spread her legs for him.

He was staring straight at her pussy.

It seemed to take him a moment to realize where his gaze had fallen, and when he looked up at her, she smiled. "Want to try shaving that, too?" she asked.

"Not today," he croaked, sounding like it was taking a severe force of will to hold himself back. "Ma'am."

Just like that, the switch flipped inside her. She reached out and grabbed his hair with her free hand, tugging him up and closer. She grabbed his right earlobe and pulled him in for a kiss while she trailed her right foot up the inside of his thighs.

"Spread your legs for me," she whispered, power surging through her. Hell, she hadn't felt this good in months. She damn sure wasn't wasting the energy.

At first, she wasn't sure he would comply. Then, his knees edged apart on the tile floor and she caressed the underside of his cock and balls with her foot.

"Such a good boy for me," she whispered.

* * * *

This…holy…fuck…

John had suspected she had something up her sleeve, but when Abbey took back control in the shower, he *felt* it. Even the air's charge shifted, her energy overwhelming him.

He couldn't deny her if he wanted to.

And damn, he did *not* want to.

He had to trust that she wouldn't do something to hurt herself.

As her toes gently stroked his cock, his sac, his eyes fell closed. She did that for several minutes before he felt her pull her foot back.

"Finish shaving my leg," she said.

She let go of his ear.

It took him a moment to gather his wits about him and open his eyes. She wore a wickedly playful smile, a gorgeous sight after weeks of pain creasing her face.

Hell, she looked ten years younger.

Her green eyes sparkled with light that had been dim for far too long.

He took a deep breath and finished shaving her left leg up to mid-thigh, as far as he could without her standing up.

Before he could start shaving her right leg, she reached out and grabbed his earlobe again and urged him to stand, bent over in front of her.

He didn't have to look to know his cock leaked pre-cum. Couldn't be helped. He hadn't been able to rub one out for several days, between his worry over her and spending nights at the hospital with her. In fact, it'd been well over a week since he'd last come. And not only was she sexy, he wanted her.

Keeping her hold on his earlobe, she pushed the showerhead into his free hand and then reached between his legs.

He let out a long, low moan as she cradled his cock and balls against her soft palm.

"I'm not a fan of CBT," she said. "But I bet you'd look good in a chastity cage."

He swallowed hard. He had one or two of those in his collection. He wasn't fond of wearing them, but he'd had past partners who'd enjoyed using them on him. "Yes, Ma'am," he said.

"But not today. Didn't you say you normally walk around naked at home?"

"Yes, Ma'am."

"Then from now on, unless you're in Sir mode, or Tilly's here, or something like that, I think I'd like it if you were naked. I want you to be comfortable."

Oh...fuck. "Yes, Ma'am." The words fell from his lips, unable to stop them.

Whatever she wanted, he knew he'd give it to her. Anything. Everything. All he wanted was her, to please her, to show her how much he loved her.

He knew that was how he felt about her. To the depths of his soul. Not just as a friend, but as way more than that.

If she'd have him in that way.

She curled her fingers around his now rock-hard cock but didn't stroke him. "I know you said we'd have a talk, but I want to do more than just talk with you," she said. "There are a lot of things I'd like to do with and to you. Things I want you to do with and to me," she said. "And times I'll want Sir to do things with and to me."

He forced his eyes open again at that, meeting her steady gaze.

"Now that I have your full and undivided attention," she said, smiling, "I want to know if you're good with that. Are you willing to switch it up with me when I need to *not* be Ma'am, and I need Sir?"

He took a deep breath and a calculated risk. He let the razor fall to the floor and cupped that hand around the back of her neck, being careful not to pull on her even as he firmly curled his fingers around her flesh and gently squeezed.

"I can be whoever, whatever you need me to be. And I'll gladly be it."

Dropping her hand from his earlobe, she leaned in and kissed him hard. But the hand around his cock slowly began stroking him, pulling a moan from him and making it difficult for him to think.

Her free hand trailed up his arm, across his chest and back again, then up to his throat, caressing. Her fingers snaked around the back of his neck and she pressed her forehead against his.

"Then come for Me," she said. "Because right now, I want to know I can make you feel good." Her fingers tightened on his shaft, her strokes quickening.

He had no time to try to hold back. He let out a gasp as his cock exploded, ropes of cum splashing across her flesh, landing on her stomach, her right thigh.

"*Such* a good boy," she cooed, not letting him go. "Such a *good* boy for Me."

John stood there, shaky, his emotions boiling inside him. Anger at himself for losing control like that, but joy that she'd demanded it of him.

Pure, unadulterated joy, for the first time in a long, long time.

* * * *

Abbey wanted to let out a triumphant cry of her own, but decided that might startle him.

Finally!

She felt strong again, in control.

Sexy.

She let go of John's cock, letting him sink to his knees in front of her. She tangled her other hand in his hair, tugging. "You need to clean up your mess," she joked. "I'm a good girl when I give a blow job. I swallow. If I swallow, so can you."

John wore a delicious, glazed subbie look in his eyes as he leaned in and started licking his juices from her flesh.

Her clit throbbed, but she knew if she tried to push him that far, to do more, that might make him balk out of fear of hurting her.

One more step forward, at least, and she was happy with that. Tom had always balked at doing this, but here was John, eagerly licking his cum off her as if his life depended on it.

Fuck. That was so goddamned *hawt*!

When he finished, he knelt there with his head laying in her lap as she stroked his hair.

"Such a *very* good boy for Me," she said, meaning it.

And she wondered how fucking damn sexy he'd be once she turned him loose on her in his Dominant mode.

"Thank you, Ma'am," he said.

"Now you can shave my other leg."

She was happy to see that when he finally sat up and handed her the showerhead, he still that subbie glaze in his eyes. This time, after he finished shaving her leg and he rinsed all the shaving gel off her, she held up her right foot, wiggling her toes at him.

Without further prompting, he started sucking on her toes, his eyes falling closed again, a look of bliss on his face.

Okay, I am going to have *to find my vibrator.*

He had *damn* good oral skills. Screw her surgical pain. She wouldn't have to move much. At this point, she was so fucking horny it would probably take less than ten seconds for her to get off. Hell, it'd been…well, since right before her fall since she'd last come.

Or…

Another plan formed in her brain.

She pulled her foot away. "We need to finish my shower," she said.

John wobbled a little as he stood, but seemed to regain his footing quickly. His cock had also started inflating again, she was happy to note.

I'm an idiot.

When they'd scened together years ago, there'd been no discussion whatsoever about sexual play. He'd asked only for impact play, hard, heavy scenes with implements and pummeling.

Had she known he was this goddamned sexy…

Fuck. I wasted four years with Tom.

No use complaining about it now.

She shifted position on the shower chair, spreading her legs, and when he started running the washcloth over her chest, she clamped a hand down on top of his over her breasts, making him squeeze as she looked up into his eyes.

"Do a good job," she said.

"Yes, Ma'am."

He took his time, working slowly. When he reached her lower stomach, she took the washcloth from him. With one hand, she put his hand on her pussy.

"Don't stop until I say you can." With the other hand, she grabbed his earlobe again. When he hesitated and started to open his mouth, she tugged on his ear. "I didn't tell you to speak."

It worked. He dropped into full-on subbie mode, and in less than a minute, his fingers had pulled the best damn orgasm of the last several months out of her.

Hell, her *first* damn orgasm in over two months.

She pulled his head down to kiss him. "Thank you. You can stop now," she said, knowing she might pay for this in a little while in terms of pain once the endorphins petered out, but feeling glad beyond her ability to say so how much it had meant to her.

He was still hard when he finished rinsing her and shut the water off. He helped her stand, wrapping a towel around her as he assisted her out of the shower.

Then he started drying her off, even dropping to his knees as he dried her legs, leaning in and kissing the top of her feet, kneeling there, waiting.

She smiled. "Such a good boy. Put my T-shirt on me and then dry yourself off."

He jumped up to get it for her, carefully helping her get it on over her head. Then he dried himself off while she watched. She reached out, trailing her fingers down his chest, over his stomach, stopping just short of the dark nest of hair at the base of his cock.

"Do you have a chastity cage?"

"Yes, Ma'am."

"Good. After you help me get settled on the couch, go get it and bring it to me."

She wanted to giggle as she watched his cute, tight ass as he ran back down the hall once she was laying on the couch with the TV on. She heard him go into the spare bedroom where their desks were and open the closet door. A little bit of rummaging, then he ran back and dropped to his knees in front of the couch.

He held up two different ones.

"Hmm." She studied her options. "Which one is most comfortable?"

He held up the one in his right hand.

"Good. Put that one on."

It took him a while to do it, because he was still hard. That made it even more fun to watch. Once the device was firmly in place, he leaned in and kissed her.

"Just remember," he said, his voice sounding thick and full of desire, "that Sir doesn't wear one of these things, and Sir just might make his girl wear the equivalent of one."

"Yes, Sir."

He smiled. "Good girl." Then he kissed the tip of her nose and walked away to get some chores done.

Holy...wow.

She didn't know if she'd just bitten off more than she could chew, but she damn sure wanted to find out.

Chapter Seventeen

Since the first morning in the shower, they'd had some discussions without getting to the meat of their relationship status issue, with more subbie time for John as he helped her bathe and shave.

Sir had even made a few appearances after gentle coaxing on her part. If John stood in front of her while she sat on the couch, his delicious cock was at the perfect height she could go down on him without it bothering her back at all.

Of course, she swallowed each time. Not that she needed any coaxing to do it, either, but it felt especially good with his hands fisting her hair while he fucked her mouth.

And every night she'd quickly dropped into sleep with John spooned around her, perfectly fitting against her body.

Whatever this was that they had, Abbey was looking forward to her back healing so she could do even more with him.

A week after getting home from the hospital the second time, she already felt worlds better than she had before her surgery despite the pain from the healing incision. They returned home that morning from another doctor check and John got her settled on the sofa to watch TV while he started doing chores.

Naked, of course.

Only four more days with him, before his vacation time ended and he went back to work the next Monday. Based on her complications, her doctor had already warned her he wouldn't think about releasing her to go back to work until at least six weeks following the second operation.

Now, more than ever, she was grateful to John for letting her move in. Even with her savings, being out of work that long would have been a struggle on her budget had she still been with Tom.

Tonight, she talked him into going to bed early. Even with him running around naked, they'd swung back and forth through the dynamic spectrum all day, between Ma'am and Sir.

She knew it was time for "the talk."

Before her head and her heart slipped too irretrievably into love with the man.

He stretched out on the bed next to her, holding hands with her. "You look like you're in a serious mood," he noted.

"Yeah, sort of." She took a deep breath. "Can we have that talk now? The big one?"

He smiled. "Cart, you left horse waaay back there."

"Yeah, I know. Seriously. Me first." She took a deep breath. "I'm not interested in sharing you with anyone."

He blew out a relieved breath. "For a second I thought you were going someplace totally different with that sentence."

"What?"

"'I'm not interested.'"

"Whoops." She giggled. "Sir can add that to His list."

This was now a running joke between them, of storing funishment points up in some imaginary masochistic cookie jar.

"He will," John said. "Believe me."

"Well?"

He kissed her. "I'm not interested in sharing you with anyone, either."

"Okay, then. That's good, right?"

"I think so."

Being with him felt good. It wasn't nearly as mentally draining as being with Tom. She didn't feel like she had to walk some imaginary line with John, staying somewhere between Dominatrix and just the dominant side of her average self to keep him happy.

Whoever she needed to be, John was okay with that.

"I've never been a switch before," she admitted.

"So? You just be you, and I'll just be me, and we'll meet in the middle wherever it falls at any particular time."

"Can I ask you something?"

"You can ask me anything, sweetheart."

She hoped he didn't take this the wrong way. "Can we hold off telling anyone about my switchy side?"

"I think Tilly already knows."

"I didn't mean her. I meant like at the club. It's going to take me a while to figure my way through this."

"You're not worried about someone hitting on you if you're in submissive mode, do you? Because, trust me, I'll knock anyone's block off if they—"

"No, that's not what I meant. I really don't know how to explain it. My whole identity with most of those people is as a Dominant. I really don't want things to get weird between me and anyone else."

"We'll handle it however you want to handle it. I'm probably more comfortable being my usual self at the club, anyway. I can keep my hood on." He smiled. "The Secret Snarker."

She gently poked him in the chest. "Yeah, well, your days of that are numbered. You really need to talk to Tilly."

"I think Tilly and I are okay," he said. She must have given him a look, because he nodded. "Okay, I'll talk with her."

"Thank you." They stared at each other for a moment. "So...this makes us boyfriend and girlfriend, right?" she asked.

He chuckled. "In the Western world, yeah, that's pretty much how it usually works."

"Okay, then." She crooked her finger at him, drawing him in for a kiss.

"So who do you want tonight?" he asked. "Sir, or sub?"

"I just want you." She reached out to the bedside table and felt around until she found the drawer. Opening it, she pulled out her vibrator. "Well, I don't think I can comfortably fuck yet, but maybe you can use this and then I'll use something else on you."

He held it up. "Been a while since I've had something in my ass. Might take me a while to get it up there." He grinned, making her laugh.

"That's not what I meant." But now that he'd brought *that* up, the thought swirled inside her brain. Something else Tom hadn't been into. No, she'd never forced it on him.

But if John liked anal…

Katie, bar the door.

"Wait a minute. Do you have a butt plug?" she asked.

"Dammit," he muttered, but the playful smile never left his face.

"*Do* you?"

He let out an exaggerated sigh. "Yes, Ma'am. I have a couple."

"Then you should go get—"

He was already up and off the bed before she could finish the sentence, making her giggle.

Oooh, this is going to be fun.

Logistically, it would be easier for him to put it in himself instead of her trying to do it and risk hurting her back. So she had him stand next to the bed, where she could watch as he lubed it and himself up and slowly started fucking the smallest one he had into his ass.

His cock stood out hard, pre-cum dripping from the slit.

Fuck, it was one of the sexiest things she'd ever seen in her life.

Once he had it all the way in and washed his hands, he returned. "Now what?"

She spread her legs and pointed at her pussy. "That. Use those oral talents on me."

He climbed up onto the bed, that quirky little smile of his making her clit throb even more. "Yes, Ma'am."

Diving in like a starving man was an apropos comparison. But somewhere along the line, after the second orgasm, he flipped from sub to Sir when she tried to push him away, lacing fingers with her and pinning her hands next to her on the bed, looking up her body and winking at her before going for orgasm number three.

And he hadn't even used the vibrator on her.

Holy…hell.

At least her mental ellipses were all good ones this time.

* * * *

John could tell from the glazed look on her face that Abbey had slipped from satisfied into subbie mode. He sat up and kissed her hard, being mindful of her back, making sure not to jostle her. But between the butt plug in his ass hitting his prostate, and eating her out, he wanted to bust a nut right now.

Inspiration struck. He grabbed the vibrator and put it in her hand, then changed position again, tossing the extra pillows at the head of the bed onto the floor and out of his way. He knelt beside her, stroking her hair before gathering a fistful of it.

"Turn it on, baby," he hoarsely said.

She did, looking up at him for further instructions.

With his free hand, he reached out and guided her hand to his cock. "Right under the glans, baby. Press it against me, and open wide."

He held her hand in position around his cock and aimed it at her mouth. He stared down into her eyes, wondering how the hell he'd gotten so lucky when his own orgasm hit.

Most of it ended up in her mouth. After he caught his breath and she shut the vibrator off, he leaned in, kissing her and licking the stray drops of his cum from her cheek.

He couldn't wait for her back to heal. Once they could do a lot more without him worrying about hurting her, he planned on spending at least a weekend in bed with her tied up and deep in subbie mode, fucking her silly and making sure she understood he'd be any- and everything she wanted or needed.

Whatever it took to make sure she understood how much he loved her and wanted her. How gorgeous she was in his eyes.

"I love you, Sir," she whispered.

He nuzzled noses with her. "I love you, too, My sweet, beautiful girl."

He removed the butt plug and got everything cleaned up before returning to bed to snuggle with her.

Nuzzling the back of her neck, he said, "And you just wait until you're feeling better. My girl is going to spend some time with her ass stuffed, too, you know."

"Dammit," she muttered, but that was followed immediately by giggles. "Yes, Sir."

"Just think, in some ways it's a self-regulating relationship. It'll keep either of us from getting too crazy, knowing the other can get payback later."

She snorted. "True. I hadn't thought about it like that."

"You're lucky I'm a soft-hearted sadist while also being an extremely heavy masochist."

A contented sigh escaped her. "Yes, Sir. You know, if you want me to beat your ass—"

"After you're healed. You're not supposed to lift anything heavier than a pillow right now, remember?"

"A riding crop isn't heavier than a pillow."

"I don't want you twisting. Believe me, when the doctor clears you to get back to activities, I'll let you make up for lost time then."

"So how do I phrase that? 'Hey, doc, when is it safe for me to hit my boyfriend?'"

He laughed. "You know Tilly would."

"I'm not Tilly."

"And that, my love, is something I'm *extremely* grateful for."

Chapter Eighteen

Four weeks post-op, the doctor cleared Abbey to do any activities she comfortably could without causing herself pain, as long as it didn't involve lifting anything heavy. She still couldn't go back to work yet, but it meant she could finally drive again, and light housework, like cooking.

She'd quit taking the pain medication the week before after tapering herself off of it the week prior to that. Now she relied solely on over-the-counter meds, relieved to be free of the heavier meds.

It also meant she and John could finally take that last hurdle and leave it in the dust. They'd made each other climax in nearly every way imaginable without it involving actual coitus and were running out of options.

After Tilly took Abbey home, Abbey set about preparing for that evening, putting a roast in the oven and getting everything ready. She thought about digging out a piece of lingerie from one of her boxes before realizing how stupid that was.

She stripped naked, walking around like that, meeting him in the hallway when he returned home.

"Well, this is a nice surprise," he said.

She led him into the living room, kissing him. "Put down the laptop."

He grinned as he left it and his lunch bag on the couch. "Is this Ma'am talking?" he asked as he loosened his tie.

She grabbed his tie before he could get it off and led him out the sliders to the lanai. "Nope. This is me talking."

It was still daylight out, but the eight-foot privacy fence meant they could run around buck naked in the backyard if they wanted. The pool was also safe. She led him to the stairs and slowly started backing down them, letting go of his tie. "Join me for a dip."

He pointed at the house. "I'm not really in the mood for a swim right n—"

"We won't be swimming. Doctor said I can do anything I want to do, except work, that doesn't involve lifting. As long as it doesn't hurt." She tipped her head toward the pool. It took him a moment to process that.

When she saw the *aha* look hit him, she smiled and nodded. "Yeah. *That.*"

He stripped faster than any man she'd ever seen, cannonballing himself into the pool before popping to the surface and swimming over to her.

She wrapped her arms and legs around him, reaching between her legs to find his hard cock, moaning as she impaled herself on his shaft. His moans echoed hers and he held still like that for a moment in the warm water, kissing her.

"Wow," he whispered. "So, so good, baby."

"Shut up and fuck me, Sir," she whispered back. When he kissed her, she roughly sucked his tongue into her mouth, her hands grabbing his hair.

He dug his fingers into her ass and started fucking her, fumbling around at first until he got them into shallower water and firmer footing.

It wasn't as good as getting pile-driven into a nice solid mattress, but it was still damn good. Good enough that when she came, she bit down on his shoulder to stifle her moans so they didn't scare the hell out of the neighbors barbecuing next door on their back porch.

"Fuck, baby," he gasped, taking a couple of last, hard thrusts inside her before falling still.

They stayed there like that, motionless for a moment. Then he began to chuckle.

"What?"

"You didn't warn me you're a biter." He kissed her.

"Is that a problem?"

"No, not at all. Feel free to dig your nails in, too. Fair warning, don't do it too soon or it could backfire on you."

"Huh? Ooohhh."

He nuzzled noses with her. "Yeah. It'll make me blow every damn time."

"Oh, reeeally?"

He arched the eyebrow at her again. "I can see my girl might need a ball gag in her mouth and leather mitts on her hands when I decide to give her a marathon fucking session."

"Promises, promises."

He led her over to the steps, where he sat on the third one down. "Come here, baby."

"What about dinner?"

"Oh, this won't take long. I've been fantasizing about getting my cock inside you for too damn long. You'll probably get several more out of me tonight, until we work this out of our systems. Hell, this is almost like the first time all over again."

"Technically, it is the first time."

"You know what I mean." He grabbed her hair and pulled her into his lap, facing him. Sure enough, he'd started getting hard again already.

This time, he settled her onto his cock, one hand playing with her nipples, the other between her legs and playing with her clit.

He nibbled and sucked on her lower lip. "Come on, girl. Give me another one."

Had sex ever been this *fun* before? Sure, it'd felt good with other people, but the sheer *joy*, that was something she could never remember feeling with anyone else.

With his hard cock embedded inside her cunt and pressing on all the right places, she let his fingers and his damn sexy voice draw her closer to release. She'd fantasized about this ever since they'd stumbled over the line from friends into lovers that morning in the shower.

Now that the moment was here, it was even better than she'd dreamed it would be. Her life was better than she thought it'd ever be. She appreciated all the moments, the little and the big ones.

She appreciated John, every last bit of him. It didn't matter how their dynamic swirled and twisted, because it was part of them and the beautifully crazy love they shared.

The second climax felt even better than her first. He swallowed her moans, fucking her mouth with his tongue while his fingers relentlessly kept her orgasm rolling through her body.

When she realized he hadn't come yet, she grabbed a fistful of his hair and tipped his head to the side. "Your turn," she whispered in his ear. "Time for you to give me what I want." She nipped his earlobe.

John muffled his cries against her shoulder. His whole body went rigid, a moment later shaking as he was wracked by laughter.

"What?"

He kissed her. "Oh, you just wait. You just wait until I can do all the dirty, filthy things I've been fantasizing about to you, girl." He stroked her back, his hands coming to rest on her shoulder blades. "I have a head full of very kinky thoughts looking for an outlet."

"You do, huh?"

"Uh-huh." He arched his eyebrows at her. "Being a switch just means double the pleasure and double the fun. I can't wait for the night I can stuff a butt plug up that sweet, gorgeous ass of yours and then tie you down and fuck you for hours without letting you come."

She gasped, liking the sound of that.

A lot.

He grinned. "But you know what I'd really like now?"

"What?"

"Dinner. I'm starving."

It was her turn to laugh. "Make you a sammich?"

"No, make me that roast or whatever it was that smelled so good when I walked in."

At least pool sex meant she didn't have to wash up. But he was a gentleman and went inside to bring her a towel so she didn't have to shiver in the AC.

As he helped her out of the pool, he pulled her in close. "Promise me something."

He sounded serious. "What?" she asked.

"If you think this is going off the rails, that *we're* going off the rails, you'll speak up and be honest with me so we can fix it. Because I damn sure don't want to lose you now that I have you."

She didn't want to promise forever yet. Hell, he knew her views on marriage.

But she also knew she didn't want to go anywhere, either.

"I promise. And ditto for you, too."

He kissed her. "Absolutely." Then he turned around and patted her on the ass. "Now get me my dinner, missy."

"Missy?"

"Ma'am?"

He was so damn cute, she couldn't help it. "I'll go get your meat, buddy."

"You already had my meat. Twice. Get me my dinner."

He made her *laugh*. All the time. Unlike—

Stop thinking about Tom, dammit!

She blew him a kiss. "Yes, Sir. I did have your meat. And it was wonderful."

"As good as you'd hoped?"

"Even better."

Chapter Nineteen

Six weeks after Abbey's surgery, it wasn't pain in her back that had Abbey on edge as they headed for Sigalo's on Saturday night. It'd be her first dinner back with the gang since her surgery. Despite frequent visitors at home, it'd be nice to get out, to see people.

To feel normal for a change.

And yet…things weren't normal. Not at all. Publicly, she was now John's Domme. After her surgery, they'd changed their FetLife profiles to reflect their new relationship statuses. Well, partially.

Privately…

Privately, tonight all she wanted to do was curl up with her head in John's lap while he stroked her hair.

Called her his good girl.

If it hadn't been for the fact that she was going stir-crazy and had missed their friends, she would have asked to stay home.

Two days earlier, she'd received a large envelope full of her mail from Tom, postmarked Dallas, that had accidentally been forwarded to him by the post office. Tony had dropped the house key off for her when Tom returned to do the move a few weeks earlier.

Not one of their friends helped Tom move.

Tilly had begged her to let her go take the key back, but as Abbey frequently reminded herself, prison orange wasn't Tilly's color.

Then, that morning while John was out mowing the grass, she'd made the mistake of logging onto FetLife to see who else had RSVP'd to go to Venture's play session that night.

She had a private message there from an acquaintance who was also friends with Tom. They'd noted the relationship shuffle and asked if she was okay.

Her strong dominant headspace fizzled.

Maybe I should have taken a page from Tilly's playbook and just reamed him a new asshole for what he did and I'd have felt better.

No, she wanted to be the bigger person. She didn't want to be some raving bitch who aired her dirty laundry all over social media.

I have a great relationship now, and that's all that matters.

Still, the sting remained. No, not nearly as bad as it had hit her at first when Tom dropped the bomb on her, but there just the same. The urge to rub Tom's face in it. That not only was there a man who was willing to go the distance for her even just as friends, but who was twice the man—in some ways literally, not just metaphorically—than Tom could ever dream of being.

Then reality took over again and quashed those revenge fantasies.

She fully expected the doctor to clear her to return to work at the eight-week mark. Part of her couldn't wait. She'd been handling e-mails and phone calls over the past couple of weeks, needing to stay busy or go stir-crazy.

After dinner, they all met up at Venture. She waited for John to get her implement bag and the cane and crop tube from the trunk before he opened her door and helped her out.

"Ready, Ma'am?" he asked with a twinkle in his eye.

She stroked his cheek. While at the club tonight, she'd be on top. Once they got home, however…

They'd developed a fun game of "flogger top." When either of them could go either way, they grabbed a flogger like kids with a baseball bat, and whoever's hand ended up at the end of the handle when it was over was "it" for the night.

It'd become a little code for them, a private game.

When they'd made the mistake of mentioning it at Tilly's one night while eating dinner there, she made them fess up.

Upon hearing their explanation, she shook her head. "As long as it's working for you two, whatever. I'll never understand you switches."

Landry cleared his throat. "Uh, love? You're a switch."

"Yeah, but not like *that*. I don't switch with *you*."

Cris cleared his throat.

She rolled her eyes. "That's different. *Duh*."

"How?" everyone else asked in unison.

Her face went red. "Give me a minute," she said, "and I'll think of something."

Abbey pulled herself back to the present. "No flogger top later tonight," she whispered. "I want Sir."

He frowned. "Sweetheart, are you all right? We don't have to play if you don't feel up to it. We can just go in and chat with everyone and go home."

"No, I want to play. But dibs on Sir tonight."

His frown meant he wasn't convinced.

She leaned in and tugged on his earlobe. "Ma'am says she's fine to play."

A smile finally broke through. "If some shrink listened to us talk, they'd lock us up. You realize that, right?"

"As long as we're locked up together, that's fine with me."

* * * *

Once they'd paid their entry fee and went inside, John headed into the bathroom to change outfits, put on the eyeliner he wore, and don his hood. Gilo had a certain look people expected. So as not to trigger more questions than they already suspected they'd get from some people, he opted to stick with his usual routine.

Abbey was scoping out equipment stations and got distracted watching a rope bondage suspension scene between Askel and Mallory. That was why she wasn't expecting it when nosy Lydia tapped her on the shoulder and leaned in, her ample bust nearly spilling out the top of her tightly cinched leather corset and into

Abbey's face.

"I heard Gilo's here tonight," she said. "I was thinking about asking him to play. You want to help me co-Top him? Get you back into the swing of things, so to speak?"

She turned to face Lydia, forcing herself to smile and not reach out and slap the woman.

She doesn't know. Remember that. She doesn't know.

"Hate to break it to you, but Gilo's not available to play tonight."

"Since when? He's like the house soccer ball. I'm sure if we ask him—"

"He's here with *me*." It took every ounce of control Abbey had to keep a catty tone out of her voice. "Sorry, but he's off the market. He only plays with me now. Guess you haven't been on Fet lately, huh?"

The thought of Lydia laying a finger on John sent creepy crawlies up Abbey's spine.

"Oh." At some point since the last time Abbey had seen her, Lydia had taken her closely cropped blonde hair into the platinum range, and it made her look older, more haggard despite her perfect nails and makeup. "Well, I *never* got *that* memo," Lydia snarked. "*Sorry.*" She turned and stomped away before Abbey could answer.

Another sheer test of her will, to not go storming after the bitch and let her have it, to inform Lydia that *sorry*, she didn't *need* to send out a fucking memo, and *certainly* not to *her*.

But at that point, John emerged from the bathroom, turning to look for her in the play space. After raising her hand so he'd spot her, he headed straight for her.

Around her neck she carried a braided leather leash, a six-footer, with snaps at both ends, allowing her to tether the pet on the other end to other items.

It had never been used on a bio-dog. Only on the two-legged kinds of pets.

When John reached her, she snapped her fingers and pointed at the floor in front of her. He dropped to his hands and knees, waiting.

Tonight he wore a leather collar he'd had for years.

I need to get him a new one. She snapped the leash onto it, tugging a little.

He nuzzled her feet, clad in black ballet flats since she didn't want to risk twisting an ankle and hurting her back in stilettos.

"Good boy." She dipped her knees enough to stroke his head through his hood.

Tilly walked up, staring down at John. "Well, Lydia's pissed off. That took less time than I thought it would." She looked down. "Hey, John."

He didn't lift his head from Abbey's feet, but he tipped her an index finger in greeting to acknowledge her.

"I forgot what a *fantastic* ass he has, Ab," Tilly said, cocking her head to get a better look at said ass. "Nicely done, girl." Tonight John wore his leather jock, leather cuffs at his wrists and ankles…and nothing else. Well, other than his hood and collar.

"As far as I'm concerned," Abbey said, her voice low and trying to keep her tone light so John didn't cue in, "Lydia can go fuck herself."

John sat up. "What happened?"

Shit. She snapped her fingers and pointed at the floor.

He sat back on his heels, hands on his knees, and shook his head. "Nope. What happened, Abbey? Talk to me."

Well, hell.

One of the things they'd discussed early on to keep things straight was that if either of them used the other's real name during play, as opposed to a title, that brought things to a screeching halt.

She felt a little funny still holding the leash as she crooked a finger for him to stand. He sometimes had trouble hearing with the hood on, and she couldn't easily bend over that far to talk to him. When he leaned in, her mouth close enough to his left ear that she could talk without yelling it to the whole club, she told him.

"Want me to go talk to her?" he asked.

"Nope. I handled it."

Tilly laughed. "Come on, Ab. Let him go talk to her. This could get interesting."

"You're not allowed to throw him under the bus, Tilly."

"No, that wasn't the deal at all. The deal was that *I* wasn't allowed to *kill* him. Nothing was ever said prohibiting me from inciting violence elsewhere." She grinned.

John turned to her and shook his head.

"Oh, fine. You two are no fun now that you're bumping uglies." But she smiled. Then she hugged Abbey. After, she pointed at John and waited. Abbey nodded, belatedly realizing what she wanted.

Only after Abbey nodded, Tilly reached up and lightly noogied the top of his head. "Such a goood boy," she said.

John gave her a playful shake of his ass.

I need to get him into puppy play. Then Abbey dragged herself back to reality. *Focus. Lydia. Warpath.*

"I handled it," Abbey said. "Let's face it, she won't be the last person to not get the memo. I'll deal with it."

"Remind me when we get home," John said, "to send messages via FetLife to the people I played with the most to update them."

"It's fine. Seriously."

"You don't look fine."

"Because Lydia's a bitch and took 'tude with me. Are we going to discuss this all night or get back to playing?"

Tilly's right. He does have a nice ass.

"Okay, if you say so."

"I do."

Abbey was more than aware of how Lydia watched from across the club, venom in her eyes when Abbey and John started playing twenty minutes later. Abbey gagged and blindfolded him, clipping his wrist cuffs to a St. Andrew's cross where she quickly stepped him up from warm-up into full-on heavy play with paddles and canes, culminating with a cane made out of a piece of Delrin hex rod with a golf club handle on the end.

She'd rarely used it on Tom.

It took two hard blows before it stood John up on his toes for a moment. She gave him time to breathe through it, waiting until he was flat-footed again to deliver a couple more strikes across his already tenderized ass with it.

This time, his fists clenched as he rose up on his toes.

She waited him out, stroking his ass until he was back on the soles of his feet again.

Then she laid one last, hard blow, right in the seam between where his ass cheeks met his upper thighs.

This time, she stepped behind him, pressing her body against his, wrapping her arms around him. "All done," she said, kissing his back, waiting for him to recover from the last strokes before unclipping his wrist cuffs.

She had left his ankle cuffs unclipped, not wanting to try to get down and back up again, and not wanting anyone's help, either. John had set her implement bag out on two chairs before she hooked him up, so she didn't have to bend over to reach things.

When he started wiggling his ass against her, she knew he was okay. She unclipped his wrists, removed the blindfold and gag, and turned him around for a hug. Normally, she'd quickly pack up the bag before getting him down, and then go to sit with him on the floor while he zoned out for a little while, surfing his subspace high.

Tonight, she needed him to wrangle the implement bag and tube. He left them next to Tilly's stuff along the wall before following Abbey to one of couches. There, Abbey took an end spot and handed him a towel to kneel on. Like that, he knelt on the floor with his head in her lap, one of her hands resting on his head, the other holding one of his.

When Lydia shot a glare at her from across the room, Abbey met it with an icy, stony gaze of her own until Lydia finally looked away and started talking to someone.

He's. Mine.

And if that scene they'd just done didn't prove it to everyone, the marks he'd be wearing on his ass for at least the next several days sure as hell did.

Abbey closed her eyes, peace filling her. It felt good to scene again. Especially with John.

I think I've finally got my groove back.

* * * *

John's ass ached in direct proportion to how his heart and soul soared. He'd be feeling that beating for several days.

Especially every time he sat down at his desk.

Behind his hood, he smiled.

He'd likely spend the next several days with a semipermanent erection during work, unable to stop thinking about tonight.

He had to trust Abbey's judgment. If she didn't want him going and notifying everyone, he wouldn't. Still, that protective part of him which would always be protective, whether in submissive or Dominant mode, wanted to have a few words with Lydia about keeping her nose out of everyone's business.

They stayed for another hour once he was up and moving again. Before they left the club, he changed back into street clothes, using a makeup remover wipe to clean off the eyeliner and running a comb through his sweat-damp hood hair. Normally, he'd go home and jump in the pool for a few minutes after scening at the club.

That was before Abbey.

Once they said their good-byes and he got her out to the car, he felt the shift in her energy immediately, not needing any verbal cues from her to know she was ready for Sir to come out.

He pulled her in for a hug next to the car. "I'm going to take My girl home, and we're going to have a nice soak in the hot tub before we go to bed and I make you come and then we go to sleep," he whispered in her ear before opening the car door.

"Thank you, Sir," she mumbled against his chest.

Confirmed.

What he wasn't expecting, when he got her home and started undressing her in their bedroom, was to discover how wet she was.

Maybe they wouldn't even make it to the hot tub.

He slowly fucked her pussy with two fingers. "Now, how did *that* happen, I wonder?" he teased.

She kept her face pressed against his shirt, holding on to him. "I can't help it. I like beating your ass. Tilly's right. You have a nice ass."

He tipped her chin up to face him, kissing her, sucking on her lower lip, nibbling, making her gasp as he sped his hand up until he knew she was close to coming—

And then he stopped. She gasped, her eyes flying open. "No."

There was his girl, in full submissive headspace.

He backed her toward the bed and nibbled on her earlobe. "Don't worry. I'm going to take care of you."

He lowered her to the bed, her ass at the edge, before gently pressing her legs apart with his. They'd experimented with a few positions that didn't hurt her back, and like this, with him standing, he could hold on to her hips and fuck her almost as hard as she wanted him to without it hurting her.

He unfastened his belt and his slacks and shoved them and his briefs down his hips. His cock sprang free and he fed it into her pussy, slowly, knowing he wouldn't take long to explode.

Something else he used to do after bottoming and springing up frisky on the other side of it, he'd come home and rub at least one, if not two out.

Before Abbey.

He took it slow, using a finger on her clit to build her back up again, wanting to time it as close as he could, wanting to come with her. When she let out a cry and he felt her pussy spasming around his cock, he quit holding back. With his hands on her hips, he fucked her, relishing the pleasant ache as his balls drew up tight against his body just before exploding and filling her with his cum.

Winded, he braced himself with his arms on either side of her.

Then she stroked his head.

He quickly turned his face to kiss her hand. "No flipping me back," he sternly said. "You earned Sir for the rest of the night."

From the guilty way her lower lip caught under her teeth, he knew that had been her plan. "How'd you know?"

"Because you're sneaky." He kissed her. "And," he added in a lighter tone, "you have no reason to feel guilty for wanting to spend the rest of the night on the bottom." Carefully, he untangled himself from her. "And if you try to be sneaky like that again, you might end up with a butt plug up your rear end all night long."

Now she pouted. "You wouldn't do that to me, would you?"

"In a heartbeat. Try me."

Her gaze narrowed. "I think you would."

"Now you're seeing things my way."

Her eyes suddenly widened.

"What?" he asked.

She grinned. "That means…"

"Dammit," he muttered.

Her grin widened. "Hey, fair's fair. Just one more thing for Ma'am to add to her box of tricks."

"You're lucky I can't spank you yet. You just wait until I can. You'll be a lovely shade of ouch, too."

She giggled. "Matching his and her bruises?"

"Absolutely."

Chapter Twenty

It was four months post-op. Over the past week, Abbey had received four calls from Tom. Each time, she sent it to voice mail.

Each time, Tom had hung up without leaving a message.

If he has something he wants to say to me, he'll have to nut up and do it. I won't make it easy on him.

She still hadn't checked out Tom's movements on FetLife beyond initially making sure he didn't have her listed on his profile once she'd moved out.

He didn't.

She refused to let herself wonder how long his profile had been like that. She didn't visit the site very often. For all she knew, he could have taken her off weeks before he actually dropped the emotional bomb on her.

Other than adding John to her profile, and checking local events, she didn't seek out Tom or his new flame. Or to see if Tom's new relationship had flamed out.

She didn't care. And she'd blocked Tom's profile so he couldn't perv her profile from his. Wouldn't stop him from creating a new profile from which to perv on her. Considering she mostly used the site to keep track of the Suncoast Society munch dates, or things going on at Venture, and rarely posted anything on the site other than congratulating people when she saw they'd posted good news, he could knock himself out. If she caused him aggravation by blocking him, that was fine with her.

She was even beyond it stinging her pride when people who hadn't been to Venture lately asked her what had happened, what was going on, and why the *hell* was she now with *Gilo*, of all damn people?

That last question in particular made her smile. She liked that there was not just one entire life—John's vanilla one—but his second life as her Dominant that only she was privy to among most of their friends.

That he had no secrets from her, and she had none from him.

That she was the only other person who knew about his painful childhood.

She was proud to be there with John, to be his Domme, to be his submissive, but most importantly, to be life partners with him.

It didn't escape her notice that she felt far closer to John than she'd ever felt to Tom. In retrospect, it had nothing to do with her. Despite Tom's claims that she'd changed…no, she hadn't. Not before the day he'd dropped the bomb on her. She wasn't doing much different now than she had with Tom.

If anything, she'd been more reticent with John than she had with Tom, her emotional scorching at Tom's hands freshly burned into her soul. Especially at first.

Tom had always tried to steer their dynamic the way he wanted it to go. Doing the things he wanted to do, asking for the things he wanted. With very little concern about what it was she wanted as his Dominant.

A do-me sub.

That difference was like night and day with John. He only asked when those conversations came up. Otherwise, his entire existence outside of work had been to take care of her and her needs, without her asking most of the time, either as a submissive or a Dominant. Learning her likes and dislikes in a way she realized Tom never had. When Abbey said something, even if just in passing, John took it as law unless she changed it.

No reminders needed, no goading, no prodding to get something done. And, no expectations of her. He was a self-starting submissive.

The energy levels she needed to be John's Domme were far different, much lower than she'd needed for Tom, who sometimes liked highly scripted scenes that took more emotional energy out of her than she'd ever realized before now. Playing with Tom had always drained her.

Playing with John replenished her emotional batteries.

And George liked him. That didn't hurt at all. John appeared to genuinely like George, too, and was always making improvements to Tortoise Town. It seemed like every day he added something, expanded it, improved it.

Other than initially helping her assemble George's enclosure, Tom had limited his engagement to washing out food and water bowls after Abbey got hurt.

Not to mention every time she turned around, it seemed John had bought some little tortoise or turtle knickknack to add to their home. And he'd gone on Etsy and bought George a costume, a little crocheted shark fin specifically made for tortoises from a vendor who made other costumes for tortoises.

He'd also long since unpacked all her boxes from the move, blending all their belongings.

Moving many of her clothes into the master bedroom.

Their lives, much as their dynamic, were enmeshed in such a way that while they were two distinct and whole people, they mixed and merged, sometimes with no clear delineation where one ended and the other began.

For her part, Abbey loved it. In her heart she felt this was her forever, the way it should be, even if she never married John.

John lived for that quiet, ever-present service, even though it benefitted him, too. Cooking and cleaning and making sure her laundry was folded the way she liked it folded, not just folding it however he wanted.

The effortless way he could step into Dominant mode himself when she needed him. How even in his service and submissive mode, that same dominance also occupied everything he did. Before this, even though Abbey knew plenty of switches, she'd never thought of herself as one. She'd assumed herself to be a Dominant after spending time as a submissive when she first entered the lifestyle.

Maybe I just needed the right man to flip my switchy switch.

John definitely fit that bill.

It was a Saturday night when they headed off to Venture. They had been working out in the yard and missed the weekly dinner at Sigalo's when they got distracted shopping online for new plants for George's enclosure.

They arrived at Venture a little after nine o'clock. Tilly spotted them almost immediately when they walked through the door, and came over to give them both hugs before getting distracted by someone else. Then Abbey helped John lace up his leather hood. He still wanted that extra level of protection for his identity when he was going to bottom to her at the club. He'd already applied the heavy kohl eyeliner before they left the house.

She wouldn't deny there was something sexy about watching him get ready, the way he almost had a ritual about it.

Maybe one day she'd feel comfortable subbing to him at the club, but not yet.

She wanted to get to that point. *If* John was willing to Top her in public.

Hell, first they'd have to break the news to her friends so they didn't get bombarded with questions about it when they did.

They were standing and talking with Seth and Leah, Abbey holding onto John's arm, when from the upstairs play space they heard the sound of a violet wand and a vibrator both shut off, followed by female moans that turned into screams of frustration, and then by muttered male swearing.

Tony walked by. "Hey, Gilo, can you give us a hand? I think something just blew up there. And not in the good way."

Now that Abbey looked, she saw a couple of smaller lights that were usually lit in the upstairs space weren't on, either.

"Sure," he said, turning to Abbey. She spotted his smile under his hood. "May I?"

She patted him on the cheek, loving the way the leather of his hood felt soft and warm under her hand. "Have fun, engineer dude."

He leaned in and kissed her before following Tony and Seth upstairs.

Tilly walked up. "What happened?" She looked toward the upstairs area.

Leah laughed. "I think someone got interrupted mid-play."

"I think someone got interrupted mid-orgasm," Abbey said.

"Dammit, I *hate* it when that happens," Tilly said. "That's just not right."

"The club's electrical system is a sadist," Leah said. "Who knew? Tease and denial."

The women laughed, watching as upstairs the men started moving things to get to the electrical circuit panel to figure out what had happened.

Abbey's attention was focused up there when she felt a hand on her shoulder.

Not thinking anything of it, she turned, then had to clamp down on a startled scream of anger.

Tom.

Standing there, as handsome as ever, with that slightly playful, slightly mischievous look he'd wear when he was angling for a spanking by being bratty on purpose.

She'd always hated when he did that. She'd known better than to reward the behavior, but sometimes it was easier to give in than to go through what needed to happen, a talk, followed by genuine discipline of the not-fun kind, like having him hold a quarter against the wall with his nose or something appropriately childish for a grown man acting like a child.

All these thoughts flitted through her mind at the same time she realized how dumb she'd been to waste those years with Tom, when during that time the perfect man, a *real* man, had been right under her nose.

"Hey, Abbey."

"Oh *no* you *didn't*," Tilly growled, lunging.

It took Abbey and Leah both struggling to hold her back before Cris and Landry saw what was going on and ran over to grab her.

"You fucker!" Tilly screamed, kicking out at Tom and narrowly missing his nuts as she twisted in her men's arms. "You goddamned son of a bitch, you *dare* show your fucking face *here* after what the hell you did?"

"I came to talk to Abbey, not you, Tilly."

"Fuck you!"

"Guys," Abbey said to Cris and Landry, her heart racing. "Please, get her out of here before she…" Wait, *why* was she making them hold her back?

Right. Prison orange is not *Tilly's color.*

She turned back to Tom, forcing her own fists to unclench. "So you're here. What do you want?"

"Can we go somewhere private and talk?"

"No." She crossed her arms over her chest and stared up at him with full-on Domme 'tude. "You want to talk, we do it here."

"I tried to call you a couple of times."

"I know. You never left a message."

"Why didn't you pick up?"

"Because I didn't want to talk to you. What do you want?"

Tilly still ranted and raved, but Landry must have tossed Cris on the sword and made him cover her mouth with his hand, because her voice suddenly sounded muffled. Abbey didn't turn to see.

"Look, I'm back in town for a week to do some stuff. I wanted to see if we could get together and talk. I have a great job out there. I could afford to move you out there with me."

Even Leah, who normally provided an even keel to Tilly's ferocious temper, made what sounded like a growl from where she stood next to Abbey.

"So what happened to that woman you were going out there to meet?" Abbey asked.

Here he had the decency to look embarrassed. "It didn't work out. She was looking for someone to support her. Not a partner."

"How ironic."

"Look, please, can we go and talk? I'm sorry. I was wrong to leave you—"

John spoke up from behind Abbey. "You're goddamned right you were."

Abbey turned. John, his hood off and in his hand, stormed over between them, getting in Tom's face as he herded Tom back and away from Abbey.

John's voice dropped, sounding low and dangerous. "Tom, you need to turn yourself around and get the fuck out of here before I do something that's going to require a lot of stitches on your part, and a lot of bail money on mine."

Holy...fuck!

If it hadn't been for the fact that they were in the club, Abbey would have ripped John's pants off and either blown or fucked him silly right there. She knew her panties had instantly soaked through, her clit throbbing at his commanding tone of voice.

Tom, clueless as always, made the mistake of smiling. "Gilo?" He let out a laugh of disbelief. "*Seriously?* What the fuck are *you* going to do? I'm here to talk to Abbey, not you. I don't know what the hell you think you're going to—"

John dropped the hood, grabbed Tom by the shirt, bodily lifted him, and slammed him into the wall, holding him a good couple of inches off the ground.

"Because," John said, "she's *mine*. You don't talk to her, you don't fucking call her, you don't so much as *look* at her without *my* permission."

"What the—"

John slammed Tom against the wall again, cutting him off. "Do you understand me?"

Abbey finally realized John was about to seriously cross a line. Cris let out a yelp of pain and then Tilly screamed, "Let me *go* so I can help John *kill* the son of a bitch!"

That finally broke Abbey's paralysis. She rushed over to John and grabbed his arm. "*Please*, don't do this," she begged. "He's not worth it."

John finally let Tom go, dropping him.

Tom, however, didn't know when to stop running his mouth. "I've got news for you, asshole. You're only a goddamned sub. *She* can tell me what she wants. This is between me and her, *not* you."

John grabbed Abbey, a fist in her hair and his other on her chin, his eyes boring into hers. "Tell him who you belong to, *girl*."

She nearly came right there, staring into John's eyes. Right now they looked dark green, like a deep, shadowy forest.

This man is seriously *getting laid when we get home.*

"I belong to *You*, Sir," she said, forgetting that the rest of the club even existed.

Around her, she belatedly realized that except for the music, the club had gone silent and still, everyone watching the confrontation play out.

"Holy fucking shit," Tilly said. "Abbey's turned full switch!"

* * * *

Oh, fuck. I'm sooo getting beaten in the bad way when we get home.

John kissed Abbey, hoping she'd forgive him for outing their other sides like that in front of everyone. He hadn't meant to do it, but the sight of Tom had enraged him so much, and then the brass fucking balls the guy had, that it just poured out of him, unbidden.

When John tried to release Abbey, to salvage the situation, she wouldn't let go of his arm. It was only when he felt the downward pressure, her tugging on his hand, that he realized she wanted him to help her onto her knees.

"I'm *Yours*, Sir," she said, looking up at him. "This girl belongs to You. And You know what? I don't care who knows it. I'm done worrying about what anyone thinks. I'm Yours, and you're Mine."

His cock hardened in his pants.

Okay. So when we get home I'm fucking her first, then *she can beat my ass.*

It'd be worth every goddamned cane stroke.

He stood next to her, his hand fisted in her hair, her cheek pressed against his thigh, and stared at Tom.

"She is *my* slave. And I'm hers. We belong to each other. Any questions, asshole? Or should I ask Landry and Cris to let Tilly loose? You have *no* idea the revenge fantasies that feisty little nurse has been cooking up for you, and frankly, I'd love to see her kick your goddamned ass."

Tom looked from Abbey to him and back again. Finally, Tony and Seth pushed their way through the crowd that had gathered, grabbed Tom by the arms, and hauled him toward the door leading out to the lobby.

Only when Tom was gone did John look down at Abbey, almost afraid of what he'd see on her face.

He didn't expect the sublime, peaceful smile.

He knelt in front of her, cradling her face in his hands, and kissed her. A round of applause started at one end of the room and before long, everyone had gathered around them, congratulating them.

"Sorry I outed us, baby" he whispered.

She smiled. "Wasn't exactly how I'd envisioned breaking the news to everyone, but turns out I'm good with it."

He stood and helped her to her feet as Tilly hurried over, Landry and Cris following.

Cris was cradling his left hand against his chest. "She fucking bit me, Abbey. Someone owes me."

"Oh, shut up, you big baby," Tilly scolded, throwing her arms around Abbey and John. "I didn't even break the skin. Not like I have rabies or something."

"Are you sure?" Leah teased.

Tilly kissed Abbey on the cheek, then John. She smiled up at him. "You know, I think I like you."

"You think?"

She let out a laugh, then wrapped both her arms around him for a crushing hug. "Hey," she whispered in his ear. "I have an image to maintain. Can it be our little secret?"

He laughed, releasing her so she could turn and focus on Abbey. Tony and Seth returned and got a quick rundown on what had started the fracas.

Leah handed John his hood. "You dropped this." She wore a playful smirk.

"Yeah, I took it off up there while we were looking at the circuit panel. I couldn't see what I was doing with it on." He ran a hand through his hair.

"Hey," a man yelled down from upstairs. "If we're copacetic, and no one's getting killed or anything, can someone please come up here and either fix the electrical system, or wait here with her while you give me a ten-minute head start before you untie her? She's pissed off her orgasm was interrupted. And that makes her really fucking mean."

Laughter roared through the club. "We'll be right up," Tony called. He and Seth started that way.

John managed to get back to Abbey through the throng of well-wishers that surrounded them. "You know, sweetheart, I think we've had enough excitement for one night."

She pouted. "Aww. I was hoping now that they know our little secret, we could both play."

He hesitated. "You sure?"

An evil little smile filled her face. "Payback's a switch. I'll beat your ass, if you'll beat mine. Sir," she added.

He grinned. "Sounds like a plan to me, girl."

He bottomed first to her, a fun, frisky scene that got her motor revving.

When he got up from the spanking bench, he skipped his Zen time and didn't even bother changing outfits to top her. He grabbed her by the hair, tipping her head back as he nuzzled her neck. "Ready for Me, girl?"

"Yes, Sir," she gasped.

He had her strip before leading her, hand in her hair, to the bench and laying her across it.

"Such a good girl for Me," he cooed in her ear, sending shivers up and down her spine.

She suspected he would go light on her, and he did, still worried about a stray hit hurting her. He used his bare hands, mostly, and a riding crop, light and on the sensual end of the scale before he rooted around in her bag and found a vibrator she'd forgotten she even had in there.

"Oh, baby. You're screwed." He twisted the base and it came on, humming in his hand. With one hand planted in the middle of her shoulders, he worked it back and forth along her clit, until she finally came for him.

This time, it was him cuddling her post-scene on the couches, once he'd put their gear away, with her wrapped in a blanket and her head in his lap.

From somewhere, she heard someone say, "So who was on top?"

Inwardly, Abbey giggled.

Yes.

Chapter Twenty-One

Three months after that event, on a Saturday morning, Abbey awoke to find John lying on his side, propped up on one arm and smiling down at her.

"What?"

"Don't *what* me," he teased, leaning in to kiss her. "I can't believe our day is finally here."

She reached up and touched his nose with her finger. "I've been thinking about something."

His smile started to fade. "Thinking, or rethinking?"

"Rethinking, but not in the way you're thinking," she said. She laced fingers with him and brought his hand to her lips, kissing it. "How about in a year, if we're still good with how things are going, that we talk about…things."

"What kind of things?"

"You know…things. Like maybe fixing it so George isn't a bastard anymore."

When John finally realized what she was talking about, he burst out laughing. "You mean make an honest woman out of you?"

"Yeah. That."

He rolled on top of her, pinning her hands over her head. "Miss Rockland, one year from today, would you do me the honor of discussing marriage with me?"

She nodded. "Yes, Mr. Gilomen. I would be honored."

When he leaned in and kissed her, she felt his erection swell between her legs. "Hey, stop that." She tried to shift her hips away from him. "We don't have time."

"Stop what?" he teased, grinding against her.

"Oooh, you're sneaky. I'm going to lock you in a chastity cage today if you aren't careful."

"Gotta catch me first," he said, almost getting his cock worked inside her. She knew if he did that she'd be a goner. Sir would come out and she'd merrily go along with whatever debauchery he wanted to do to her.

I'm such a slut for him.

Not that it was a bad thing, but when Tilly had both a key and the alarm code to get in, the last thing Abbey needed was her best friend walking in and interrupting their sex.

She snuck her right hand free and grabbed his left earlobe, pinching it and pulling his head down. "What did you say?"

His body fell still, even his voice changing to that delicious subbie tone she loved hearing from him. "Sorry, Ma'am."

"Now, unless *you* want to call Tilly and explain to her why we're running late, because *you* wanted to flogger top this morning, you'd better roll off me so I can get my shower. Because I know I damn sure am *not* going to try to face her down today of all days. And get me my coffee, please."

He let out a sad sigh. "Yes, Ma'am." Then he kissed her, rolling off her. "She is determined today will go perfectly. Even I wouldn't try to backtalk her today."

"Exactly."

Abbey was in the shower fifteen minutes later when she heard the bathroom door open.

"Why the *hell* are you still in the shower? We're supposed to be at the hair salon in forty minutes!"

Then, John's voice. "Honey, Tilly's here."

"Thanks for the warning," Abbey said. She poked her head out from behind the shower curtain. "I'll be done in five minutes."

Tilly turned on John. "This is *your* fault, isn't it? Did you distract her with sex this morning?"

"No," Abbey said, saving him. "He didn't. He was a very good boy for me this morning."

John sent her a wink and blew her a kiss before disappearing from the doorway.

Tilly, however, leaned against the counter, waiting. Abbey resumed her shower, knowing trying to get Tilly out of there would only unleash her on poor John.

"You know, I'm glad I was wrong about him," Tilly said.

"Did you just admit you were wrong about something?"

"Yeah, yeah, I know. Mark the calendar and all that bullshit. Believe me, Landry and Cris are still yukking it up that I like John."

Abbey was glad the shower curtain hid her grin. "Thank you for not killing him," she said. "Because I love him."

"Well, I certainly *hope* you love him, after all the shit he's been through for you."

"What's that supposed to mean?"

"Not like *that*. I meant how worried he was about you."

Abbey poked her head past the shower curtain again. "What?"

Tilly was in serious mode. She dropped her voice. "At the hospital. He was worried sick about you." She rolled her eyes. "Sooo...*okay*. When I saw how he was there, how he took care of you, how upset he was when you, you *know*..."

Tilly sighed. "I knew back then John was the right guy for you. I can't possibly imagine Tom ever getting his self-absorbed head pried out of his ass long enough to take care of you the way John has. *Okay*?"

"Why didn't you ever give me your opinion of Tom before?"

"Because for starters, you never asked. And you never let on there were any problems. I mean, I thought he was okay, but when you compare the way John is around you to Tom, it's like trying to compare the best filet out there to some gristly ground beef."

"Ick." She pulled her head back in to finish her shower. "Thanks for *that* mental image."

"Hey, you asked. And John's ass is a lot nicer than Tom's."

"True."

She'd no sooner shut the water off than Tilly thrust a bath towel through to her. "Thanks."

"Hurry. Up. I don't want us to be late."

"It takes ten minutes to get there from here."

"Uh, *yeah*. Hence why I don't want us to be late."

She finished drying off and wrapped the towel around her before pulling the shower curtain open. "Okay, so honest opinion. What do you think about John?"

"I thought I just told you."

"Seriously."

Tilly dropped all pretense and walked over to her. "If you don't put a ring on that man's hand in the next couple of years, I'm gonna have to get sneaky, drag you both to Vegas, get you two drunk, and you'll sober up to the sounds of an Elvis impersonator telling John to kiss his bride, meaning you." She smiled. "I know you're gun-shy, but hey, I think he's the real deal."

"So what do you have up your sleeve for today?"

The Cheshire Cat would be proud. "Oh, a little fucking payback for all the times he's bugged me. Take it as a sign of how much I love the guy that I even care." With that, Tilly turned and left the bathroom.

"Oh, fuck," Abbey muttered.

* * * *

No matter how Abbey tried, Tilly wouldn't fess up. And if she'd told Leah, Loren, or any of the others, they didn't spill the beans, either. Finally, after shepherding Abbey through hair and nails and makeup and getting her dressed in her new corset and skirt, Tilly drove her to the club for the ceremony.

At first, Abbey didn't see John. She had the silver bracelet she was going to put on him as his day collar, but she didn't know what he was giving her.

If Tilly knew that info as well, she wasn't saying.

When they first arrived at Venture a little after five thirty p.m., she noticed several groups of people clustered here and there in the club, looking at their cell phones interspersed with various giggles and amused looks.

"Where's John?" Abbey asked Tilly. "You didn't lock him up somewhere, did you?"

"Nooo. Landry and Cris are bringing him shortly." She craned her head around to look at the clock on the wall. "They're due any time. Hey, the invites said we're starting at six, so that's when we get started."

Abbey also noticed that when people saw her, they were hiding their phones.

"Til, you know John can't be photographed by anyone, right? Just Kel."

"No one's going to photograph you two but Kel."

"Then what's everyone doing with their phones out?"

"Never you mind."

Shit.

Abbey knew. It had something to do with Tilly's revenge. She wasn't sure what, but…something.

Tilly marched her up to the front to stand and wait with Loren. Abbey handed the jeweler's box off to Loren, who'd give it to her when it was time. When Tilly headed off to handle something, Abbey leaned in.

"Fess up. What's the deal?"

Loren grinned. "Oh, nothing. Why do you ask?"

No help there.

She didn't have any more time to think about it. Because then Cris entered, followed by Landry…

And John.

Oh...my.

He'd also kept it a secret from her what he'd planned to wear. Now she understood why. The black tailored suit fit him perfectly. He wore silver cufflinks in his white dress shirt, and the red, black, blue, and silver striped tie reflected the colors of the BDSM flag. He was freshly shaven, and his hair perfectly styled.

When he walked up to her, her pussy throbbed, her clit aching to feel his tongue.

Abbey had been to weddings and collarings in this club, from casual to tuxedo formal.

Never had she seen a man looking as handsome as John did at that exact moment.

The corner of his mouth quirked in a smile. "You like?"

She nodded, speech beyond her at that point.

She *loved*.

"Okay, kiddies," Tilly said, herding everyone into their seats. "Time to get this show on the road." She headed up to the front of the room to stand behind Loren.

"What are you doing?" Abbey whispered to Tilly.

Loren smiled. "Don't worry about it."

Abbey looked up at John and saw him smiling, too. "You're in on this, aren't you?"

He shrugged.

Askel got into position and took a few pictures of Abbey and John standing in front of Loren, Tilly sliding out of the way to avoid being captured in the frame.

Loren cleared her throat, and the audience settled down as John and Abbey faced each other and joined hands. "Well, here we are again, folks," Loren said to a smattering of chuckles. "And would you believe of all people who is standing in front of us today? Uh, not meaning you, Abbey."

Tilly held up one finger behind Loren. Abbey turned to look at the audience in time to see over half of them hold up phones. From them blared Jack Nicholson's famous line from *The Shining* as he burst into the bathroom with an ax.

"Heeere's Johnny!"

The audience exploded with laughter.

Abbey looked up at John. He still wore that smile.

"You knew!" she whispered.

He shrugged. "Tony made Tilly an app and she had people download it. He asked me. I could have said no, but why spoil her fun?"

Shit.

When they settled down again, Loren continued. "These two have been through a lot to get where they are now. As we all know too well, they came very close to having a not-so-happy ending."

Abbey glanced at Tilly, who smiled but didn't move.

John squeezed Abbey's hands to focus her attention back on him.

"So today is about humor, and celebrations, and loving life," Loren continued. "Because, as we all know, that's what makes it so good."

Tilly held up two fingers.

From the audience blared part of a really dirty military cadence from the movie *Full Metal Jacket*. The attendees laughed at the, "Mmm good," part and didn't stop until Loren looked back to Tilly for help. Tilly raised her hands to settle them down.

When Abbey looked up at John, she realized he was desperately trying not to burst out laughing.

Hell, she'd been worried about crying and ruining her makeup. Not laughing herself out of her corset.

Loren continued, giggling her way through the next few words until she pulled herself together.

"Most of the ceremonies we have here follow a fairly standard pattern, even though they're all unique. Usually, there's a Dominant and a submissive, or some variation thereof. But Abbey and John go beyond that, two switches with a fluid dynamic. If any of you have ever watched their scenes, you know what I mean when I say it's a joy to witness what they do, and how they seamlessly switch things up when they play."

Tilly held up three fingers and a line from *Spaceballs* blasted, about going from suck to blow.

Okay, even Abbey had to laugh at that one.

"Some people might not get what they do," Loren continued, "and that's all right. Because their brand of crazy is just that—theirs. And it only has to matter to them."

Tilly held up four fingers.

Maniacal giggles filled the room, making the audience members burst into laughter again.

Abbey arched an eyebrow at Tilly.

"There's only one more," Tilly whispered. "Chill."

"Abbey," Loren said, "your turn. Ladies first."

She smiled up at John. "You've seen me at my worst, were there at my darkest time, at the lowest point in my life. I had friends there, but you were so much more. I wish it hadn't taken me so many years to find you. I feel you're my home, where I should have been all along. I want to share this life with you as friends, lovers, partners, and more. I hope I've earned your trust to be your Owner, the way you've earned my trust to be mine. You own my heart, my love, and my body. Will you take this and wear it as both my owned and my Owner? My slave and my Sir?"

He smiled. "It will be my honor and my pleasure."

Loren handed her the jeweler's box. From it, Abbey withdrew the bracelet and fastened it around John's right wrist. Then she kissed his palm, pressing it to her chest. "I love you."

"I love you, too, sweetheart."

Abbey glanced at Tilly, but she only smiled.

Loren said, "John? Your turn." She handed him a jeweler's box.

He took it, pausing for a moment before turning back to Abbey. "I've spent my life compartmentalizing. Separating the things that wouldn't mix well. Vanilla from kinky, even though service is, for me, an integral part of who I am, although it doesn't look like that to the casual observer. You're the first person in my life to bring all those pieces together, to shatter those walls and show me how good life is with the right one. I love you, and want to spend the rest of my life with you. Owned by you, owning you. Life is too short for fear when happiness is staring me in the face. I want to be happy, and I want to be happy with you. Will you have me, owned and Owner? My slave and my Domme?"

She hoped she didn't start crying. "Yes. Please."

He opened the box and inside lay a gorgeous gold heart-shaped pendant with pieces of amethyst. She held her hair out of the way so he could fasten it around her neck.

"Now before we close this ceremony out and hit the wonderfully delish food trough over there," Loren said, "I think Tilly has one more thing to add to this."

Tilly grinned. "We now pronounce you switch and switch." She shook her fist in the air. From around the space, the sound of whips cracking echoed from the phones, spurring one last round of laughter, as well as applause.

John pulled Abbey to him and kissed her. All she wanted to do was go home, but knew to leave without hanging around with everyone would be rude.

Especially considering the reason they'd all come out early was to see them and witness their collaring. It took forever to get hugs and congratulations from everyone. Tilly waited until the end.

"So was that it?" Abbey asked.

Tilly grinned. "Yes. And I promise at your wedding I won't do that. I'll behave myself."

When John made his way back to Abbey and slipped his arm around her waist, she leaned in.

"I have a request," she said.

"As my Owner or My girl?"

"Yes."

He chuckled and stopped walking to turn to her, his arms around her. "Yes?"

"You know I said I wanted to talk about stuff in a year?"

"Yeeesss?"

She snuggled more tightly against him. "How about we make that six months, so that we can plan in advance and have our wedding on the same date?"

With his hand cupping the nape of her neck, he leaned in and kissed her, hard and long and melting her thoroughly. "Yes, baby," he whispered. "I think that's a damn good idea."

Chapter Twenty-Two

When they got home, John hurried around the car to open the passenger door for her before grabbing their bags out of the trunk. He unlocked the front door and got the alarm shut off, holding the door for her and smiling as he waited for her to go through first.

Abbey wouldn't deny excitement and desire coursed through her. Tonight they could fully be who they wanted to be, everybody getting their needs filled.

Among other things.

"Where do you want the implement bags, Mistress?" he asked.

"Bedroom, please. Wait for me there. Get naked."

He hustled them off to the bedroom while she kicked off her shoes and walked into the kitchen to get herself a glass of water. She had a little surprise for him tonight.

Well, not little.

And she knew damn well that payback was a switch…and so was John.

If he waited until tomorrow night to extract his revenge, she'd be surprised.

When she walked into the bedroom, she found him on his hands and knees on the floor.

Naked.

She grabbed a fistful of his hair and tipped his head back. "Who's my good boy?"

"Me, Ma'am."

"That's right. Up on the bed. On all fours."

She didn't let go of his hair until he'd positioned himself on the towels. She patted his ass. "Good boy. Wait right there."

He wiggled his ass at her in reply, making her giggle.

She found the cane she wanted in her tube and laid it on the bed. Then she retrieved the gloves, lube, paper towels, and butt plug from the bathroom that she'd hidden there ahead of time.

Oh, there would be some payback from him on the other end of this, all right.

She could only imagine what he'd do.

And the thought made her pussy wet. It was sure to be fun, regardless.

Pulling the gloves on, she squirted lube onto her right index finger and slowly started massaging it into his rim.

He moaned, his head dropping to the bed, cock hardening. "Oh…fuck," he whispered.

"That's right. Someone's getting their ass stuffed with a nice, fat butt plug before I give him his caning."

Another low moan rippled through him, making her even wetter, making her clit throb in response.

She took her time working up to three fingers in his ass, pre-cum dripping from his hard cock as he slowly rocked his hips against her hand. Once she was sure she had him loosened up enough to take the plug, she withdrew her fingers, grabbed the plug, and lubed it before pressing the tip of it against his ass.

"Here we go. I'll take as long as it takes to get it stuffed inside you."

She gently pressed it against his rim, going slow, a little at a time. Press and withdraw, gaining more ground each time, until she started approaching the widest part of the plug.

"Oh…goddamn, you bitch," he muttered. His hands fisted the covers even as he slowly worked his hips in time with her movements.

"What was that?"

"Goddamn, you bitch, Ma'am," he said.

She laughed. "That's what I thought you said."

It took another couple of minutes, but she finally got it completely seated in his ass, drawing one last, long moan from him as she did.

"Holy, fuck," he gasped. "What the *hell* is that?"

She stripped the glove from her right hand, turning it inside out as she did and dropping it onto the floor for him to take care of later. She kept the left one on in case she needed it.

"A new toy I bought for you. It came yesterday via UPS."

"Oh...*fuck*. That thing's huge."

"Not too huge for your ass, baby." She patted his ass cheeks. "Feet on the floor. You know what comes next."

A thin strand of pre-cum still leaked from the slit of his engorged cock.

Oh, I'm sooo getting fucked here shortly.

She nearly giggled again.

Reaching for the rattan cane on the bed, she waited for John to get his feet firmly planted on the floor, legs spread, bent over the end of the bed. The base of the butt plug was visible between his butt cheeks. She gently pressed on it with her left index finger, making him moan again.

"How's that feel?" she asked.

"Like someone's going to get it up their ass pretty soon."

"Ah, soon, but probably not tonight," she said. "It is going to stay in your ass while you fuck me."

He groaned again, his cock visibly twitching between his legs.

She reached between his legs and gently stroked his balls with her fingers. "What's wrong? Somebody horny?"

"Yes, Ma'am." He wiggled his hips again, but his voice sounded a little slurred, like he was dropping down into subspace.

Standing on his left, she laid the cane across his ass with her right hand, her left planted in the middle of his back not so much to hold him in place but to add to his experience.

"These are going to be good ones," she said. "I heard someone say they wanted their ass caned tonight."

He rested his forehead against the bed. "Yes, Ma'am," he mumbled.

"How many strokes are you getting tonight?" she asked, knowing it was mean to make him think while he was trying to drop into subspace, but enjoying it anyway.

I really am more of a sadist than I thought I was.

"Twenty, Ma'am," he said.

"Really? I thought it was only fifteen."

"I figured I'd get some in advance."

She giggled. "You can't roll them over like cell phone minutes."

"Dammit," he muttered.

"Still want twenty?"

A content sigh escaped him. "Yes, Ma'am. It's been a few weeks."

Yes, it had been a few weeks since they'd had a real rip-roaring scene. He'd been getting his subbie fix through service to her. She'd been getting her subbie fix via sexual submission to him.

But between catching up on work ahead of their planned vacation next week and doing stuff around the house, other than the occasional quickie scene between them, the masochist side him hadn't been able to do much except sit on the sidelines and twiddle his thumbs.

Unlike with Tom, she knew John genuinely didn't mind, because he loved her for who she was, not what she could do for or to him.

She gave him the twenty, not making them all very hard ones because she was more eager to get to the fucking. She crawled up onto the bed next to him, on her back.

"How's that ass feel?"

"Like it's a lovely shade of ouch. Thank you, Ma'am."

"You're welcome...Sir."

He pounced, grabbing her wrists and pinning her hands over her head as he shoved his knees between her legs, forcing her thighs open.

"Oh, you are sooo getting fucked, girl."

"Promises, promises."

He transferred both her wrists into one hand and then reached down, fisting his cock and lining it up with her pussy. When he sank his cock into her, they both froze, letting out nearly identical sighs of pleasure.

Then he pressed her thighs up, against her chest, ankles over his shoulders before pinning her hands over her head again.

She was so glad her back had healed enough to allow this position. He could fuck her hard and deep like this. She loved feeling engulfed, pinned, owned.

He took his time, slowly stroking his cock deep inside her. "I think someone needs to get tied up tonight and spend a few hours with a vibrating egg in their pussy."

A pitiful whine escaped her. "That's not fair."

"Really?"

"Well...yeah."

"Okay, I'm curious. How do you figure that?"

"You don't have a pussy. I can't stick it in you."

"Sure you can. Just put it in a condom first and..."

She grinned.

"Dammit," he muttered, starting to fuck her a little faster. "That's not fair. That means I just need to fuck you harder and drive all that damn toppy energy out of you tonight."

Actually, he had a very good chance of doing just that by fucking her at that angle. She tried to struggle against him a little, making him clamp down even harder on her wrists.

"Where do you think you're going?"

She squirmed a little more, loving the struggle. "Nowhere."

"That's right. My girl's going to lay right there and get herself fucked."

He leaned in and nibbled on the side of her neck, his teeth grazing her flesh.

Her orgasm started instantly, her body already knowing what was coming and trained to respond to him. He bit down, intensifying her pleasure, slowing his strokes to hold back his own release as she squirmed and cried and loved every second of it.

He made her lay there while he fucked two more orgasms out of her before he finally gave in and came, filling her pussy with his cum and then collapsing on top of her.

Sated, spent, and thoroughly pleased with herself, she inhaled, loving their scent.

"This thing is fucking huge," he mumbled against her neck.

She giggled. "I know."

"I'm going to have to spend a few hours at least working you up to it."

She giggled again. "I know."

He sat up, staring down at her. "I love you."

Her smile widened. "I know. I love you, too." She had a thought. "Can we bump the talk to three months instead of six?"

"Should I just propose now and be done with it?"

"I don't know. Is there any rule about a guy proposing with a butt plug up his ass?"

He nuzzled noses with her. "No, but you might have one up yours while I do."

"Dammit," she muttered. "Hey, at least I didn't make you wear it during the ceremony."

He sat up, a wide, evil grin spreading across his face. "Dibs on making you wear it during the wedding."

"Dammit!" she said.

THE END

WWW.TYMBERDALTON.COM

ABOUT THE AUTHOR

Tymber Dalton lives in the Tampa Bay region of Florida with her husband (aka "The World's Best Husband™") and too many pets. Active in the BDSM lifestyle, the two-time EPIC winner is also the bestselling author of over seventy books, including *The Reluctant Dom*, *The Denim Dom*, *Cardinal's Rule*, the Suncoast Society series, the Love Slave for Two series, the Triple Trouble series, the Coffeeshop Coven series, the Good Will Ghost Hunting series, the Drunk Monkeys series, and many more.

She loves to hear from readers! Please feel free to drop by her website and sign up for updates to keep abreast of the latest news, views, snarkage, and releases.

www.facebook.com/tymberdalton
www.facebook.com/groups/TymbersTrybe
www.twitter.com/TymberDalton

For all titles by Tymber Dalton, please visit
www.bookstrand.com/tymber-dalton

For titles by Tymber Dalton writing as
Tessa Monroe, please visit
www.bookstrand.com/tessa-monroe

For titles by Tymber Dalton writing as
Macy Largo, please visit
www.bookstrand.com/macy-largo

For titles by Tymber Dalton writing as
Lesli Richardson, please visit
www.bookstrand.com/lesli-richardson

Siren Publishing, Inc.
www.SirenPublishing.com

CPSIA information can be obtained
at www.ICGtesting.com
Printed in the USA
LVOW04s0729290116
472464LV00019B/664/P

9 781632 590800